Modern and Classic
WOODBURNING STOVES

Box Stoves.

ENTIRELY NEW AND VERY HANDSOME.

44113—

Price, each.

22 inches, with one 7 inch boiler holes, 75 lbs. $3.25
25 inches, with two 7 inch boiler holes, 100 lbs. 3.65
28 inches, with two 8 inch boiler holes, 120 lbs. 4.80
30 inches, with two 8 inch boiler holes, 125 lbs. 5.33
34 inches, with two 9 inch boiler holes, 165 lbs. 7.50

Modern and Classic
WOODBURNING STOVES
and the grass roots energy revival

by

Bob and Carol Ross

illustrated by

Graham Blackburn

from the authors' original material

Overlook Press

WOODSTOCK NEW YORK

First published in the United States
of America in 1976 by
The Overlook Press
Lewis Hollow Road
Woodstock, New York 12498
Second Printing, 1977

Library of Congress Catalog Card Number: 76-11431
ISBN 0-87951-049-8

Designed by Graham Blackburn
Printed in the United States of America

ACKNOWLEDGMENTS

We would like to thank the many people who, directly and indirectly, helped us to get this book together.

First, Peter Mayer, our publisher, who came up with the idea of the book in the first place and Graham Blackburn who designed and illustrated. Others who helped with the book are: Priscilla Ashworth, Holly Beye, Alf Evers, Dave Hubbard, Robert Joyce, and Paul Sturges. Special thanks to Erica Morgan of Maine Audubon for providing us with the material (almost word for word) on the Gilsland Farm House. Thanks also to the folks at Total Environmental Action who sent the information on the Tyrrell House.

Contributing to our background education in thermodynamics and architecture are: Barry Commoner, George Erdman, Albert Fellows, Richard Hill, Bruce Anderson, Ken Kern, John Rummler, Mike Sarco, Jay Shelton, and Paul Sturges.

For our introduction to the inner workings of the politics of energy we are grateful to: Larry Bogart, Barry Commoner, William Heronemus, Donald Hunter, John Schnebly, and Paul Sturges.

Paul Sturges wins the "hat trick" (scoring three times) for this project. He has been of incalculable assistance in helping us to get to the "nitty gritty" of things.

To a large extent, our "objectivity" in comparing different makes of stoves has come from visiting Nichols Hardware in Lyme, New Hampshire, and talking with the Nichols brothers. The Nichols family has been in the stove business for generations; they presently carry at least sixty different stoves including practically every stove mentioned in this book. We have traveled extensively throughout the New England states gathering material, and want to thank Eva Horton of Kristia Associates for helping us plan the tour.

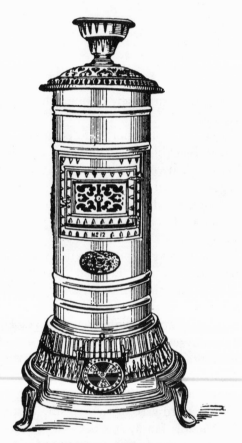

44103 Gem Windsor.

CONTENTS

CONTENTS

CONTENTS

Acme Stove Pipe.

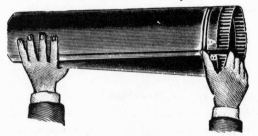

(Cut shows manner of putting pipe together.)

INTRODUCTION

The electricity went out at one o'clock in the morning, just as Andy Hopkins was checking the bolt on the back door against the blizzard-like winds that had awakened him from a brief two hour's sleep. As he rummaged in a kitchen drawer for a flashlight, he recalled the previous night's weather forecast: ". . .storm warnings, winds gusting to seventy-five miles per hour, sleet and freezing rain."

"Well, what do you know," he thought, when he snuggled into bed beside his peacefully sleeping wife, "this time the weatherman hit the nail right on the head."

By eight o'clock that morning the service was on again. Alice Hopkins switched on the morning news report as she supervised the coffee-perking and the eggs frying on the gas range. Schools were closed. The roads were too hazardous for travel; driving was advised only in cases of emergency. Over one hundred and twenty miles of the Thruway closed. Trees down over numerous local roads. Utility lines down.

She poured herself a cup of coffee and looked out the window at her favorite white birch furiously swaying in the wind. The newscaster droned on: "Here's today's forecast for our listening area. . . ." And the radio went dead and the lights went out.

Later Andy trekked the half mile to the post office, where he heard the latest news from the chatty postmaster, Ed Brooks.

"Oh, it's not some local line that's broke," said Ed, "it's something out at the central station. The whole doggone county is out! It may be a while before we get our electricity back. You know, I feel sorry for those folks in those new all-electric houses on Maple Lane. Likely it'll drop to fifteen degrees by tonight and what with this wind and all, they might as well just go back to bed and throw on some extra blankets!"

Sometime late that afternoon the storm stopped, but the power was still off at suppertime. The earlier excitement of the storm had worn off and now things were just getting uncomfortable.

Alice carried the Aladdin kerosene lamp into the kitchen. She began to methodically line up pots and pitchers on the kitchen table. With no electricity to run the pump, the only water they'd been using was what was in the pressure tank, but now there was no pressure, so they had to fill up containers from the tank directly.

"Watch your step when you're on those stairs, hon'." called Andy from the basement where he had been lighting and placing candles.

Alice glanced at the indoor-outdoor thermometer as she gathered up an armload of pots. Forty-three degrees already.

"Darn!" She hadn't counted on the oil burner going off. But there was no electricity to run the motor. Still, they were lucky they could cook. She was glad they'd decided against trading in the gas range for an electric one with a self-cleaning oven last year.

INTRODUCTION

Down in the basement, Andy and eight year old Matt were filling up pots. Matt, having taken advantage of the holiday from school, had been all over the neighborhood that afternoon.

"The Hendersons' pipes froze," he announced, "and the Rogers are having a big party at their house. Everybody is going over there."

"A party?"

"Yeah, they're cooking all kinds of stuff on their wood stove. A big stew and hot cocoa, and their house is real warm. I had some hot cocoa with marshmallows. Hey, we're invited over there, I just remembered."

Shortly, Alice, Andy, and Matt joined a score of their neighbors at the Rogers' residence. There was indeed a party going on. They gathered around the cozy old parlor stove until the power went on again at nine-thirty that night.

This story is typical of the experiences of many people each winter. Most of the events described occur with some regularity in many parts of the country. Although the Rogers' with the old parlor stove are not to be found in every suburban neighborhood, there has been a great renewal of interest in wood stoves which has touched virtually every section of the country. In fact, there are many neighborhoods where the number of woodstoves in operation might conceivably present a problem when choosing where you would prefer to visit: at the Browns' you can see the fire; the Smiths' stove is better for cooking on; the Jones' stove heats the whole house *and* you can cook on it!

The rapid increase in costs of other fuels, as well as the possibility of future shortages, has caused many people to think of going "back to wood." But this alone does not fully explain the dramatic increase in popularity of woodburning stoves.

As the demand for wood heat has grown, new types of stoves have become more readily available. These offer many improvements over the old-fashioned stoves, including more heat output with less wood, longer periods of burning, and better control of the fire. The list of advantages does not stop here, however, and there are many subtle but significant differences between the various types of stoves. When one starts to look into the matter, all sorts of questions come up and it is hard to find answers that are anything more than personal opinions.

In this book we attempt to provide the essential background information necessary to answer all the basic questions which are apt to arise. We are particularly delighted to reveal the most recently discovered innovations in wood heating, because it becomes ever clearer that we are not limited to going "back to wood" but have within our reach the possibility of going "forward to wood" in a manner which can greatly reduce our dependence on conventional fuels without abandoning the convenience of our present life styles.

CHAPTER ONE

BASIC PRINCIPLES

THE MECHANICS AND CHEMISTRY OF COMBUSTION

To understand how different stoves operate, and to know how to use any given stove or fireplace to its best advantage, it is helpful to have a practical acquaintance with the mechanics and chemistry of the combustion of wood.

Chemically, what happens is little more than a reaction involving only three basic elements: carbon, hydrogen, and oxygen. Wood is composed almost entirely of cellulose and, to a lesser extent, lignin. The chemical formula for these compounds is $C_6H_{12}O_5$. When heated, these break down into a variety of gases, liquid tars, acids, etc. This process is referred to as the destructive distillation of wood. A list of the various substances which have been evolved from the wood distillation process is given in table 1.

SOURCE: Seeley and Keator, "Woodburning Space Heaters," *Mechanical Engineering*, December 1940.

1. HYGROSCOPIC WATER	PARAFFIN
2. GAS, consisting mainly of:	PHENOL
ACETYLENE	OXYPHENIC ACID
ETHYLENE	CRYSYLIC ACID
BENZOL	PHLORYLIC ACID
NAPTHALENE	CREOSOTE $C_7H_8O_2$; $C_8H_{10}O_2$;
CARBON MONOXIDE	$C_9H_{12}O_2$
CARBON DIOXIDE	RESINS
METHANE	4. PYROLIGNEOUS ACID, consisting of:
HYDROGEN	ACETIC ACID
3. LIQUID TAR, consisting of:	PROPIONIC ACID
BENZOL	ACETONE
NAPTHALENE	WOOD ALCOHOL
RETENE	5. WOOD CHARCOAL

Table 1 PRODUCTS OF WOOD DISTILLATION

Combustion occurs when the more volatile of these distilled gases are mixed with air at temperatures high enough to ignite them. Depending on what is reacting to what and under what conditions, new molecular compounds are created during the combustion process. This becomes rather complicated and is not well understood, so perhaps we can go back to the beginning and look at the basic process more closely.

In burning wood, the first thing that must be done is to raise its temperature. At 250°F. any moisture in the wood must change into steam before the temperature will rise any further. Most well-seasoned firewood contains about 20% moisture. This is why it takes a while for a fire to "catch on." After the steam has been driven out, the temperature can once again rise until, at about 380° F., the distillation of gases begins. It is very important to understand that initially it is only these gases which burn. The wood itself does not burn at this stage. Furthermore, not all of the gases do burn; some are non-combustible and some of the most prevalent, such as carbon dioxide, actually smother volatiles and prevent them from combining with fresh air and igniting. This is one of the basic facts which accounts for such wide differences in efficiencies obtained when burning wood under various conditions. To the extent that we can get all of the volatile distillates to combine with fresh air at temperatures high enough to cause ignition, we shall achieve maximum efficiency and top performance from our heaters.

In a moment we will examine how this is done. First let's finish looking at the combustion process.

As the volatile gases combine with oxygen and ignite, the temperatures continue to rise. Most stove fires achieve maximum combustion temperatures of between 1,100° to 2,000° F., although higher temperatures are possible.

These various stages of combustion do not occur uniformly, by the way, but proceed first at the surface level of the wood being burned and gradually work their way into the center. Thus we will find that gases are burning at the surface while an inner zone is still losing its moisture and the center part of the log may be just starting to warm up.

During the gas-burning phase, heat is produced chiefly through released hydrogen combining with oxygen. When this stage of combustion is completed we are left with charcoal, which is mostly carbon. This solid fuel burns more slowly and evenly, providing a good deal of heat. If not used to raise the temperature of fresh fuel, these coals will continue to gently radiate heat for many hours, especially if they are protected from the cooling effects of excess drafts.

The protection of the fire from cooling is the most important consideration in achieving good efficiency. In later sections you will notice that it is the airtight stoves which, having the best control over draft, give the most heat for the amount of wood burned.

MAXIMUM EFFICIENCY OF COMBUSTION

Now that we have described the basic stages of simple combustion, let us examine how a fire can be engineered to obtain maximum efficiency. Actually we are not so much interested in getting the heat out of the wood as we are in getting it into the house. All wood has a certain heat potential which must be released before its combustion is completed. The trick is to get as much burning done as possible before the smoke goes up the chimney. Theoretically, if we achieve totally complete combustion, there should be practically nothing going up the chimney but carbon dioxide, water vapor, and a trace of carbon monoxide. Applied to most wood burning appliances this goal remains approachable but not attainable. We have mentioned complete combustion of volatile gases and protection from excess cooling as the essential conditions for optimum efficiency. This is true but there is a catch! If wood is burned at hot enough temperatures, say 3,000° F., with plenty of air, combustion would be complete. The catch is that this would normally require such a great deal of air rushing through the stove that a considerable amount of heat would be carried out the chimney. A simple solution to this problem would be to install a heat exchanger on the chimney but the effectiveness of a heat exchanger is somewhat dependent on its resisting the air flow and this would, in turn, tend to limit the rate of air flow and lower the combustion temperatures. A better understanding of this relationship can be obtained by referring to the section on heat exchangers later in the book.

On the industrial level, there have been solutions to this problem. In Berlin, New York there is a plant that manufactures wooden knobs and flower picks. All of the scrap wood (beech and white birch) is shredded into coarse sawdust and is literally exploded as fuel in enormous kilns. The heat is converted to steam in large heat exchangers and the steam drives turbines which can provide almost all the electricity needed to run the plant. The entire operation is run by a bank of computers. Attempts are being made to engineer results on a smaller level.

Mr. Paul Sturges, a heat-recovery specialist, of Stone Ridge, New York, is working on a wood heat system designed for off-peak storage, to be used at the Cary arboretum in Millbrook, New York.

Professor Richard Hill of the University of Maine has designed a similar wood heat furnace system to be used as a supplemental heat source in a solar house being built by the Audubon Society near Portland, Maine.

The relatively high rates of firing required by these systems also entail infrequent firing and that the heat released be stored by some means in order to be evenly and continuously distributed to the living area. While we can try to apply the principles of total combustion to our selection and use of wood burning stoves, it is most likely that we shall have to compromise on efficiency at some point when considering convenient operation, appearance, cost, etc. Most people can understand the "put another log on the fire" approach. Nevertheless, knowledge of the principles of efficient combustion can lead to the putting of far fewer logs on the old fire.

SUMMARY

Normally fires do not burn very efficiently. This is due to the cooling effect of excess drafts and the lack of sufficient air distribution to burn all the distilled volatile gases. Keeping excess drafts from a fire can make it possible to retain at least 50% of the heat released by the fuel. At higher temperatures even more heat will be released. If, in addition, there is secondary combustion of volatiles, net efficiencies of at least 60% can be achieved.

Significant amounts of heat can be saved from the 40% going up the chimney by the use of a heat exchanger. Theoretically, it is possible to get quite close to 100% efficiency but, in practice, any heat exchanger recovering half the heat passing through it, is doing pretty well. So we can expect a maximum of 80% efficiency if we want to go to that extreme. Compared to the 25% efficiency we have grown accustomed to with old-fashioned type wood stoves this is a great deal more heat for a lot less effort. Even if one does not agree that wood warms you twice (once when you cut it and once when you burn it), in today's unpredictable energy market, an acre or two of good hardwood trees can put a lot of warmth in your life.

CHAPTER TWO

SELECTING A STOVE

WHAT TO LOOK FOR

What is it we want? If we are to be satisfied with what we get, we must decide before we buy just what it is we want and ask also if what we would like corresponds to what we need. There are six main things to consider.

1. Function

Basically, this means what *type* of stove. A cookstove will serve as a heater but its primary use is for cooking. For looking at the fire there are many different styles of free-standing fireplaces. Franklin type stoves can be used for viewing the fire, or their doors can be closed to radiate more heat. A new type of stove, Combi-fires, offers the same fire-viewing features as Franklins but are heaters of exceptional efficiency whether open or closed.

Heating stoves are divided into two general types according to function: radiant or convective. The difference is that a radiant stove simply radiates the heat directly to people and objects around it, while a convective stove is usually a radiant inner stove surrounded by a cabinet, and heats the air rising between the stove and the cabinet. Convection heaters are more useful in situations where more heat is wanted on the floor above, such as in basements. Radiant heaters are better for large open spaces and where comfort is desired at lower air temperatures.

2. Appearance

This can be tricky. The idea is to determine how well the stove will fit in with its surroundings and your sense of taste. It is often difficult, when looking at a stove, to picture how it will look in your home. A good technique is to keep looking at the stove and closing your eyes until you can retain a mental image of it. Then visualize how it will look *when hooked up* and operating in your home. Try and imagine everything you can about what it will be like. Will you have it on a hearth? Will you keep wood stacked nearby?

Alan, a friend of ours, bought a thermostatically controlled stove, one of the more functional-looking models. His wife, Cindy, saw it for the first time when it was delivered to the house. She was very dismayed by the starkly utilitarian appearance of the stove. Finding it difficult to control her agitation, she gracefully left the house for the day, leaving Alan and the installer to hook up the stove. When Cindy returned the stove was connected to a new stainless steel chimney. It looked much better, somehow, connected to the stovepipe and sitting on a bluestone hearth. A fire was built but, as it takes several hours for a new stove to get its full heating capacity built up, and even longer for the warmth of a stove to work its way into a large house, our friends went to sleep that night not entirely sure how things were going.

We were curious ourselves and called them the next morning. Cindy answered the phone and I asked her how she felt.

"Warm!" she replied. I had never heard the word "warm" sound so luxurious. Our friends had just kicked a $200 a month electric heat habit.

Cindy later confessed that when the stove first arrived it reminded her of the ovens of Auschwitz. After a week of getting used to round-the-clock wood heat, she felt like the stove was a member of the family.

This is all that needs to be said to illustrate the value of using some creative thought in anticipating how a particular stove will fit in to your decor.

3. Durability

As a rule this is directly related to the price, but there are some significant open considerations. The big debate is over cast iron versus steel. The problem is that each of these materials is durable in a different way. Cast iron has many good qualities but its durability relies on the fact that it is very resistant to deteriorating or deforming under most firebox temperatures. It does tend to be brittle and will crack due to rapid changes of temperature, differences in temperature, or from a sharp blow such as might be caused from throwing a log into the stove too energetically.

Steel, on the other hand, is malleable, which means that it will not crack like cast iron. However, it will deform and break down more rapidly under fire. Some stove manufacturers have tried to overcome this shortcoming by using thicker steel, but the very best stoves, whether of cast iron or steel, make use of interior panels to protect the firebox. The best material for this is "refractory" or firebrick. Other materials used are cast iron, aluminized steel, stainless steel and heavy steel plate. While these linings protect the stove to some degree, they are still subject to the short-comings previously mentioned. The advantage is that if they are damaged they can usually (but not always) be readily replaced.

4. Safety

Generally stoves do not present nearly as great a fire hazard as a poor stovepipe connection or a careless owner. The safety of the installation will be discussed later. As a rule, the more massive and durable a stove is, the safer it is. There can be little doubt that a cabinet type would give the best protection against accidental burns. When buying a stove, check closely such things as how securely the door latches.

5. Cost

"I'll gladly pay you Tuesday for a stove today." By all means do not overlook the possibility of financing a new stove. In today's energy market a wood stove is one of the best investments you can make. Quite often the cost of both the stove and the installation is repaid in a single heating season. A stove with a less expensive sticker price can often wind up costing more after a year or two of operation than a more efficient model. The smart buyer will amortise the stove by dividing the cost of the stove by its life expectancy. This tells you how much your stove is costing you each year. To this you add the amount you would have to spend for firewood each year if you used that stove, remembering that different stoves will do the same job using different amounts of wood, depending on the efficiency of the stove. *Other things being equal, a more efficient stove will repay almost any additional cost in time.*

For example, suppose you are trying to decide between a thermostatically controlled stove costing $300 which operates at an efficiency of 50%, and a cast-iron box stove costing $150 but which is only half as efficient as the other stove. Assume that it will cost $300 to install a chimney for either stove and that the thermostatically controlled stove will require $50 worth of replacement parts every ten years whereas the box stove should last indefinitely. Taking 25 years as an average mortgage time, we can compute a yearly cost of $28 for the thermostatically controlled stove and a yearly cost of $18 for the box stove. You are now in the position of asking yourself if you would rather spend $10 more a year for your stove or come up with several extra cords of wood.

6. Effectiveness

How well will the stove do the job you want it to? This is perhaps the most important consideration in buying a stove. The effectiveness of a stove is determined primarily by its size. It is obvious that a very large space cannot be heated by a very small stove, and, with but few exceptions, you would not want a large stove in a tiny room.

Once you have decided what size stove you need, the efficiency is the next logical consideration. How much heat will it deliver (usually measured in BTU's per hour) and how long will it burn? How well can you control the draft? Is there a provision for secondary combustion of volatiles, and to what extent does the secondary combustion actually occur under normal operating conditions? Many stoves with "secondary combustion" features are seldom fired hot enough for *any* secondary combustion to take place. Much can be learned from the weight of a stove. Generally a more massive stove is more efficient, but only if the weight contributes to keeping the combustion zone hot. The best stoves will combine a very hot firebox with a good heat exchange surface as the gases are leaving the stove. This latter is not too critical since you can add your own heat exchanger to the stovepipe.

While not affecting the basic efficiency of a stove, a removable ash pan is a welcome addition.

HEATING ONE OR TWO ROOMS

If you are looking to heat the garage for four hours each Saturday morning, an inexpensive stove is appropriate. There are numerous sheet-metal box stoves on the market in the $50 price range. Since these light gauge stoves can quickly warp to the point of being inoperable it is advisable to shop for a nationally established name brand. This will give you the best assurance that people like yourself have bought the stove in the past and have been sufficiently satisfied with its performance to recommend it to others and to buy it again when it finally wears out (light gauge metal stoves do wear out quickly). At the present time there have been so many cheap stoves "engineered" by short-of-work sheet metal fabricators that a good deal of caution is advised in buying (or selling, and especially in making) such merchandise.

Another inexpensive stove that is really quite durable is the converted oil drum stove; 100% cast-iron conversion kits are available. They cost about $50 and consist of a door and its frame, a set of legs, and a stovepipe collar. You provide your own fifty-five gallon oil drum, and simply cut out the required openings and attach the fixtures. You can usually obtain a used fifty-five gallon drum for a few dollars.

It is also possible to make your own conversion kit from scrap metal; a bit of skill with a cutting torch etc., is all that is needed to ensure that the stove will function well.

Oil drum stoves are bulky, and will throw off a considerable amount of heat. It is a good idea to be sure you can give them plenty of room before buying one. The one conversion kit we know of is made by the Washington Stove Works.

The best-established name brand stoves we know for light use are cylindrical stoves made of light gauge blued steel, such as the Autocrat-Pine Wood, or the Reeves. These give the most trouble-free operation and are about the least expensive stoves to be found anywhere.

For a stove that is to be used regularly, most people would prefer something with a little more substance. Domestically manufactured cast-iron box stoves and pot-bellied stoves are still being made. Models suitable for heating small areas are attractively priced from $100 to $150. Used ones, if you can find them, are in the same price range and might well be a better buy if they are in good working order. Check closely to be sure the doors fit tightly. There should be no cracks or missing pieces.

There has been a drop in the craftsmanship of American made iron stoves during recent years, especially in the larger foundries. This has not been necessarily intentional on the part of the manufacturers; numerous problems have arisen which have been very difficult to deal with, such as a tightening of environmental quality standards and the strict requirements of the Occupational Safety and Health Act.

One company that has maintained exceptional quality of workmanship is Washington Stove Works, one of the oldest and finest stove foundries in the country. Their stoves are all made from beautifully designed original patterns and good quality iron, neatly finished. The Arctic box stove, made by Washington Stove Works, will heat at least two rooms. It holds a sizable load of 22" logs, and features two removable cook plates set in a top which is itself removable, although normally one would load the stove from the front door. Other cast-iron box stoves are made by Portland Franklin Stove Foundry, Fawcett Division of Enheat Ltd., and King Stove & Range Co. (see appendix I for addresses).

In a convertible fireplace-heater type stove, Washington Stove Works makes the Olympic Franklin in the 22" size, which is just right for a single room. An 18" model, which might be nice in a bedroom or someplace where an occasional fire would be cozy, is just a trifle small to rely on for steady heat. Incidentally, the sizes of Franklin stoves (18", 22", 24", etc.,) refer to the distance across the front of the

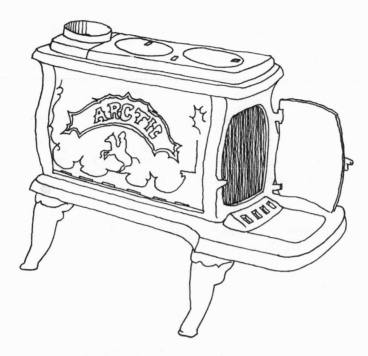

Figure 1   ARCTIC BOX STOVE

opening. The overall width of the stove is usually several inches more, and the length of logs that will fit is usually several inches less.

All the cast-iron stoves mentioned so far may be considered as a class with very similar functional characteristics, advantages and disadvantages. We shall refer to them from now on as "traditional American cast-iron stoves." Although they cost about twice as much as their sheet metal counterparts, they are at least ten times as durable as light gauge sheet metal stoves. Cast iron has a reputation of being a better radiator of heat, but we have not noticed any appreciable difference in the *amount* of heat thrown by a cast-iron stove as compared to a steel stove of similar dimensions, unless the iron is cast in such a way that it has a greater total surface area (as is often the case with European cast-iron stoves).

Much of the engineering of the traditional American cast-iron stoves has been directed towards developing models of attractive design. Efficiency has taken the back seat. Approximately 75% of the potential heat in the firewood will go up the chimney leaving only 25% to heat your house. While this is much more than is provided by most fireplaces, much is left to be desired, especially since these stoves cannot be run for more than two to four hours without the fire going out.

During the last few years, increasing numbers of cast-iron box stoves of European manufacture have been imported to this country. They have become so popular so rapidly that skeptics have coined the phrase "the wood stove fad," as if frequent reference to this incantation would make these foreign-looking little things go away.

Such antics fail to give proper credence to the underlying motive for the popularity of these stoves: dwindling oil and gas reserves and endlessly rising fuel prices. It is likely that this "fad" will develop a history more similar to pizza pie than to hula hoops.

The chief advantage of the European stoves is that they can be fired overnight leaving sufficient coals the next morning to start a new fire simply by adding more wood. They operate at twice the efficiency of the traditional American cast-iron stoves, which means that you can get the same amount of heat out of them using half as much wood. Most of them are made of very high quality iron, and they are very tightly assembled and sealed against unwanted drafts.

Suitable models for heating one or two rooms are the Jøtul 602, the Trolla 102 and 105, both Norwegian makes; the Lange 6303A and the Morsø 2B, both made in Denmark; and the Chappee 8008 and 8033, from France. These stoves cost from $250 to $350, the more expensive models having a deep baked enamel finish in a selection of attractive colors.

The Chappee deserves special mention because there is considerable difference between the two models, although they appear to be very similar. Both models are of enameled cast-iron construction with a hinged top, opening to a smooth cooking surface. Both models have a small eisenglass window through which the glow of the fire can be seen.

Model 8008 is fed through a side-loading door and is meant to burn wood only. It takes wood up to 16" in length and will burn for eight hours between loadings. There is an inner lining of sheet metal, or cast iron where the Chappee engineers have seen fit, and the base of the stove is lined with fire brick. As with most cast-iron box stoves, the ashes must be shoveled out the fuel loading door.

Model 8033 has two front-opening doors. The upper one is for loading the fire, the lower one is for providing access to a removable ash pan. This model is fully lined with high quality refractory brick and has a heavy duty shakable cast-iron grate. Additionally, there is a built-in heat exchanger which allows hotter combustion temperatures to be maintained without losing the heat up the chimney. It is designed to burn both wood and coal. For wood burning it takes 15" logs and may burn up to seven hours at a loading. Do not be misled by the small size or plain styling of the

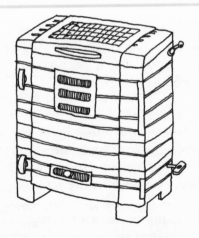

Figure 2   CHAPPEE 8033

Chappee, it is one of the more ingeniously designed of the European stoves and its front-opening doors make it ideally suited for installation inside an existing fireplace.

Due to a lack of sophisticated promotion, and perhaps because of the simple, unadorned styling, people have been slow to warm up to the Chappee wherever it has been newly introduced. The model 8033, however, is a really fine stove which deserves serious consideration. If used strictly for burning wood, it is hard to imagine that it would ever burn out.

Of all the European stoves, none has been as popular as the Jøtul 602. Its design appeals to almost everybody's taste. It is available in either a painted black finish or a high-gloss baked enamel in a forest green color. It features interior baffle plates to protect the sides against excessive heat, and an interior top baffle plate which directs the products of combustion into a special chamber for greater heat transfer. The round cooktop is cast with special fins on the underside, which tend to conduct more heat up to the cooking surface. Wood up to 16″ in length is loaded through the front door. It will go up to eight hours between loadings; we have heard of its going more than twelve hours, although it is questionable whether it was producing any great amount of heat for such a long run (the owner claims it was).

Figure 3   JØTUL 602

The Trolla 102 and 105 are so similar to the Jøtul as to be considered copies, which very well might be the case. There are a few notable differences. The Trollas are only available in black finishes. The 102 is a very small stove, suitable for only one sizable room. It takes 12″ long wood. The 105 is of a similar capacity to the Jøtul 602, taking 16″ lengths of wood. The bottom and sides of this model are lined with firebrick. There is a difference both in design and workmanship between the Jøtuls and Trollas; generally the Jøtul appears to be more neatly made. One person's taste may differ from another's, however, and some people do prefer the Trolla.

The Danish stoves have appeared on the scene more recently than the Norwegian makes. Already the Lange is starting to sell as well or better than the Jøtuls in many stores. The quality of workmanship is comparable but the Lange has two advantages. First, the design is decidedly more classicly Hellenic — which seems to be more appealing to American taste. Second, the enameled models are available in a wider variety of colors: blue, red, green, brown, and black. Functionally, the Lange 6303A performs about as well as the Jøtul 602, although there is no interior baffle plate. It will take wood up to 20″ in length, and can go eight hours between loadings.

Figure 4   LANGE 6303A

The Morsø 2B, another Danish make, is equipped with a top baffle and secondary air chamber similar to the Norwegian stoves. In addition there is an added smoke flap above the door to reduce smoking during loading. This is but an extra precaution since you would not normally load the stove while it was smoking. Generally, the castings of the Morsø are thinner, but this does not necessarily mean they will weaken sooner. They are available only in a mat black enamel finish. They accept logs up to 20″ in length and can burn for eight hours or more at a single loading.

HEATING SEVERAL ROOMS

Both the traditional American cast-iron stoves and the European cast-iron stoves mentioned earlier are made in larger models with correspondingly larger heating capacities.

24

Franklin stoves sized from 26″ on up are priced from about $375, complete with grates and screen. Imported Franklin stoves are available in these same sizes at considerably lower prices. Some of them are outright copies of American stoves. The quality of the cast iron in these imported Franklins is virtually anybody's guess. Keep this in mind and also consider the possibility that replacement parts could be difficult or impossible to obtain in the future.

Washington Stove Works, mentioned in the preceding section, make two top quality pot-bellied stoves of decent size, which will burn either wood or coal. They also manufacture a parlor stove available with varying degrees of fancy nickle-plated trim. It is one of the most beautifully designed stoves on the market. Wood up to 24″ in length is loaded through the side door. The front door, which is equipped with eisenglass panels, can be removed completely for viewing the open fire. There are two cooking plates on top of the stove which can be used, although certain types of cooking (rapid boiling, for instance) would require a pretty hot fire.

Figure 5   OLYMPIC PARLOR STOVE

Prices for the Olympic parlor stove range from $300 to $450 depending on how much nickle plate you want. If you consider these prices intimidating, remember that the Arctic box stove, mentioned earlier, will put out enough heat for several rooms. It just has to be loaded more frequently. The same would hold true for any sizable cast-iron box stove. Don't forget that most box stoves, parlor stoves and pot-bellied stoves will burn twice as much wood as airtight models.

Other Franklin and parlor stoves are made by Portland Franklin Stove Works, Fawcett Division of Enheat Ltd., and Atlanta Stove Works (see appendix I for addresses).

The European manufacturers have provided two different approaches to heating a larger area. One is simply to offer a bigger version of their smaller box stoves. The Norwegian Jøtul 118, the Trolla 107, and the Danish Lange 6203BR and 6204 are priced from $350 to $500. Once again, the enameled stoves are more expensive than the plain black models.

Figure 6   JØTUL 118

The Jøtul 118, like the smaller Jøtul 602, is equipped with cast-iron baffle plates. Unlike the 602, which can be vented from the top or back, the 118 offers options of venting from the back or from either side. There is no cookplate in the top, but the entire top will lift off for cleaning. It is gasketed with asbestos rope, which keeps it tightly sealed. Occasionally, these tops will warp (less than a 10% chance) so be sure the dealer will be able to get a free replacement quickly from the importer. The 118 burns a 24" log for up to 12 hours. It is available in green enamel or black.

The Trolla 107 is a bigger version of the Trolla 102, having the same sort of cast iron baffles as the Jøtul, but with a fixed top and cooking plate. It vents from the top or back and takes up to 24" lengths of wood.

The Danish 6203BR and 6204 are more properly considered parlor stoves than box stoves, although they are actually a little of both. The most striking feature of these stoves is their highly ornamental design which resembles the styling of the old European tile stoves. They are fully protected by baffles on *all* sides as well as on top. The hand-filed door provides an airtight seal without the use of gaskets and has two separate draft controls. The door is located far enough above the base of the stove to permit ashes to accumulate for a week or more before removal.

WOOD BURNS SLOWLY FROM FRONT TO BACK LIKE A CIGARETTE

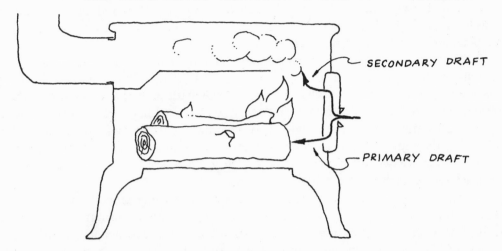

Figure 7   HOW MOST SCANDINAVIAN STOVES WORK

Figure 8   LANGE 6203 BR

The model 6203BR takes a good sized load of 16″ wood and will burn up to ten hours between loadings. Model 6204 takes up to 22″ wood and will burn up to twelve hours. Both models are available in plain black painted finish or in high gloss blue, green, red, brown or black enamel.

Another design for increased heating capacity employed by Europeans is an additional heat exchanger on top of a smaller stove. The Morsø 2BO and the Lange 6203 are simply the smaller models 2B and 6203A with arch-shaped heat exchangers mounted on top. Due to the fact that the gases have a longer path to travel before they are discharged from the stove, these chambers extract and radiate more heat while using the same amount of fuel. Therefore, they not only offer a greater heating capacity but increased efficiency as well. These units are somewhat less expensive than the larger models (118 & 6204).

Some people will discern that a very similar "shaker stove" can be made by adding a few extra twists and turns to the stovepipe. This is absolutely correct. Be mindful of a tendency for increased formation of creosote when improving the efficiency of a low-draft, airtight stove. Creosote will be less of a problem when the stove is being run full-blast. For this reason we like the versatility of the stovepipe approach. You can use a direct pipe run during mild weather and install a heat exchange section in colder weather (see figure 38).

For people who would be satisfied with the efficiency of the European stoves without paying the extra money for the fancy cast iron work, Larry Gay, in Marlboro, Vermont, has demonstrated that Americans can do some ingenious copying of foreign stoves. His Independence stove is made of 3/16″ steel plate with interior baffle plates, and has secondary combustion features almost identical to the Jøtul 118. Priced around $300, it is also available with exterior soapstone baffles, for about $75 extra, which convert it to a combination radiant-and-convection stove.

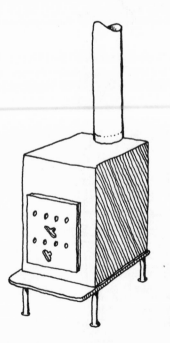

Figure 9   INDEPENDENCE

Other steel stoves based on the Jøtul design are made by Sunshine Stove Works, and Ram Forge (see appendix I for addresses).

The Alaskan is another American-made "no nonsense" box stove. According to the manufacturer, its 1/4" and 5/16" steel plates won't warp, bend, buckle or stretch. It is lined with firebrick and is priced around $300 and takes 18" wood.

An interesting steel stove is the Tempwood. This is a true downdraft combustion stove which achieves excellent efficiency. Loading is a bit awkward, the only access being through the top cook plate. Removal of ashes is even more difficult, since the fire must be allowed to go out before the ashes may be hauled up through the top opening. Fortunately, this chore need not be done more than once a month. The Tempwood sells for around $240.

There are numerous stoves with automatic thermostats which are certainly the most intriguing stoves for heating larger areas. The best known is the Ashley 25HF, also known as the Columbian. This stove is a rather surprising crossbreed of a light gauge double-wall sheet metal body, with a cast-iron top and fuel door. Martin Industries, makers of the Ashley, also produce a very similar stove, the King 6600A. This differs from the 25HF but slightly. It has a solid cast-iron bottom, which the Ashley does not, but the workmanship is less carefully executed than with the Ashley. Watch out you don't buy one with a warped top!

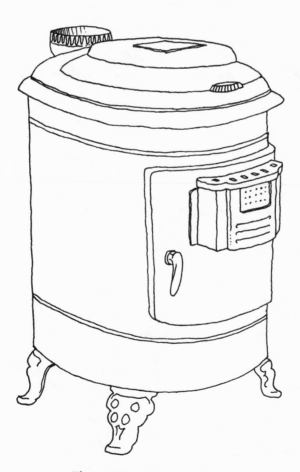

Figure 10   ASHLEY 25HF

29

It is becoming more apparent that the Ashley's popularity has been due to its relative availability and, until recently, the dearth of decent competition. Many people have complained of operating difficulties with this stove. We would like to think that it functions well if equipped with the patented downdraft equalizer, installed properly and operated intelligently, according to the principles that will be explained in the section on installation. However, it is evident that the stove is sufficiently finnicky to be in need of further engineering improvements.

The Ashley Console model is a convection-type heater which consists of a steel inner stove equipped with cast-iron liners and grates, surrounded by a cabinet. It burns about the same as the Columbian and, once it is working right, will heat three to four rooms with decent efficiency. Several other companies have copied the Ashley cabinet design, namely: U.S. Stove (Wonderwood model 26) and Autocrat (Thermo-Wood). The features of these stoves are identical to the Ashley Imperial, which will be discussed in detail subsequently.

The Riteway model 2000 is a very high performance and thermostatically controlled stove which can comfortably heat even a good-size house. There are two things which make this stove a good choice also for a smaller area. One is the relatively inexpensive price — around $300. The other is the full-on/full-off effect of the magnetic damper, which makes the Riteway operate at the same high level of efficiency no matter how small or large the heating load. We shall discuss this stove more fully later on.

Other thermostatically controlled stoves, such as the Shenandoah model R55 and the Thermo-Controll, can be used in small areas. The Shenandoah has firebrick linings, which is nice, but it does not seem to be as well-engineered for consistent top performance as some of the more well-established stove makes.

HEATING AN ENTIRE HOUSE

Most of us can easily accept the concept of a large room, even a few sizable rooms, being heated by a woodburning stove. But the idea of one wood fire providing all the heat needed for an entire house can be a bit more difficult to comprehend.

In times past, if a house were heated by wood, a number of stoves were usually employed. People who can still remember such scenes invariably recall a woodburning kitchen range, and parlor stoves in more rooms than just the parlor. As we have pointed out, however, stoves have changed. Additionally, our homes are smaller and much better insulated. As a result we find there is a great variety of wood stoves capable of serving as central heating systems for most houses. There is a wide difference in the capacities of these various stoves, and there is an equal difference in the requirements of different houses. For the sake of accuracy, therefore, we shall, in this section, identify as nearly as possible the maximum amount of living space which the various stoves can be expected to heat. This will be expressed in cubic feet (length x width x height) of houses built to current standards, and will assume that houses located in cold climates are adequately insulated. In most cases, our figures will correspond with the manufacturer's figures, but not always. The Riteway Manufacturing Company, in particular, tends to be very conservative in the claims it makes.

This may be due to the fact that it is possible to get poor results with a stove by burning the wrong kind of wood, or using a poor chimney, to name the two most common means, and Riteway just happens to be the kind of outfit that places a high value on a good reputation. Therefore, they seem exceptionally careful when allowing for less than ideal conditions "in the field."

In many respects, a stove serving as a central heating system is considered as something akin to a furnace. Indeed, the most popular stoves for this purpose are the thermostatically controlled units. Still, the deciding element is the capacity to produce enough heat and almost every make of stove we have discussed so far has at least one model suitable for the purpose.

Although the larger European box stoves can be used to heat larger areas, they would require more frequent loadings and it is questionable whether they would stand up well under such intense use. The Lange 6302A is the only box stove model of European make which can take insulated areas of over 1,000 square feet in its stride. Like the smaller Langes, the 6302A is equipped with full-length side liners to protect against the heat of the coals. Instead of an interior baffle plate, the 6302A has an entirely separate heat exchange chamber built into the top section. Baffles inside this section direct the gases past a cooking lid before they finally leave the stove through the top flue. A special hook which comes with the stove makes the Lange cook lid very easy to remove, although since it opens into the heat exchanger and not directly to the fire, we can't see why anyone would want to remove the lid while the stove is going. For best heat transfer to the cooking surface you can substitute the finned Jøtul cookplate ($16 - Jøtul dealer). The Lange 6302A takes 24" logs and will burn

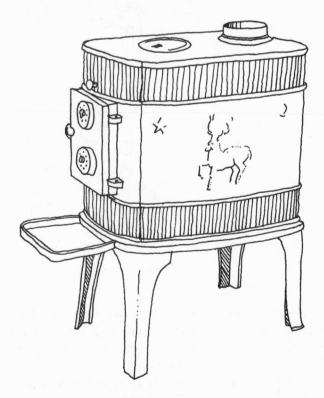

Figure 11   LANGE 6302A

up to twelve hours on a loading. It costs $450 to $500 in black and about $550 in enamel. Selection of colors includes blue, green, red, brown, and black enamel. This model will heat an area of 9,000 cubic feet.

The Sierra 200 and 300 are airtight box stoves of exceptional capacity. The 1/4" and 5/10" steel plates are guaranteed not to warp, bend, buckle, or stretch, and there is a lifetime guarantee on the workmanship. The bottom and sides of the stove are firebrick lined.

The manufacturer claims that "almost 100%" combustion is achieved through the re-circulation of the gases which occurs as a result of the flue pipe extending into the stove. In fact, the Sierra has been tested at the same efficiency as other airtight stoves, which is to say around 50% under conditions of ordinary use.

In our opinion, the efficiency of this stove is attributable to its firebrick linings and general massiveness.

The model 200 takes up to 24" logs, and will heat at least 9,000 cubic feet. It is priced around $375. The model 300 takes up to 30" logs, will heat at least 12,000 cubic feet, and costs around $400.

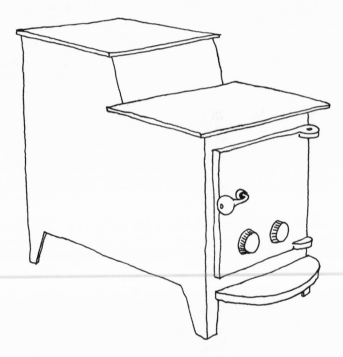

Figure 12   FISHER

Many of the various stoves discussed have been lab tested at efficiencies exceeding 70%. However, as such tests usually involve drier wood, higher rates of firing, and greater heat recovery through forced air convection across lateral stovepipe runs, these figures would not be possible in "the field" unless the laboratory conditions were duplicated. This is more than a possibility, nevertheless, and we shall discuss such conditions in the chapter on Custom Heat Systems.

As we said, thermostatically controlled stoves are the most popular for large central heating applications. The thermostat for these units consists of an adjustable bimetallic coil, which, once set, will automatically adjust the damper to maintain the same room temperature. These stoves share a number of basic similarities, yet the differences, though subtle, affect the overall performance to a remarkable degree. None of these stoves are likely to win top honors as far as looks go. Their chief attraction is their ability to heat at a reasonable cost.

The least expensive, priced between $250 and $275, is the Shenandoah R75. This is a barrel-type stove with minimum gadgetry. The top and door are made of 11 gauge steel, and the jacket is of 18 gauge steel. It is equipped with firebrick liners, and a cast-iron grate set in a cold rolled steel rim. A cast-iron rim is available as an option and we strongly endorse its use. Because the combustion air is admitted through the grates from below, there will most likely be many times when the hot coals will come into contact with the rim. Under these conditions, cast iron will undoubtedly last much longer. The R75 takes the prize for largest fuel door. This is quite handy, but it does increase the possibility of warping. For this reason the door

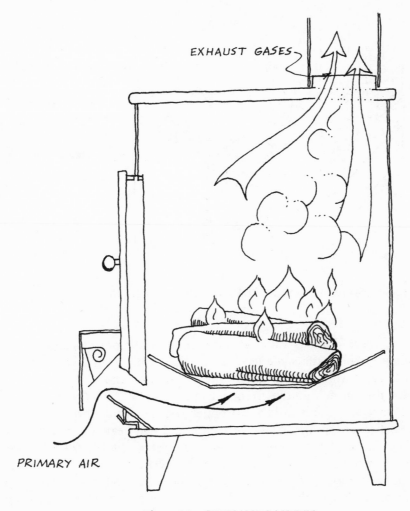

Figure 13   SHENANDOAH R75

has been structurally double-reinforced. This stove will take larger sizes, but 16″ to 18″ seems to be the optimum length of logs. It can heat up to 12,000 cubic feet and will go 12 to 24 hours between loadings.

The Ashley Imperial is a larger version of the Console model, previously mentioned. This is a convection-type heater, consisting of a steel inner stove, with cast liners and grates, surrounded by a cabinet. Air is admitted near the top of the stove and drawn down a preheating channel to be distributed at the level of the firebed. This appears to be advantageous, although it is questionable how much improvement is realized by warming the combustion air 50° or so when the temperatures of combustion are in the vicinity of 1,000°. Still, every little bit helps.

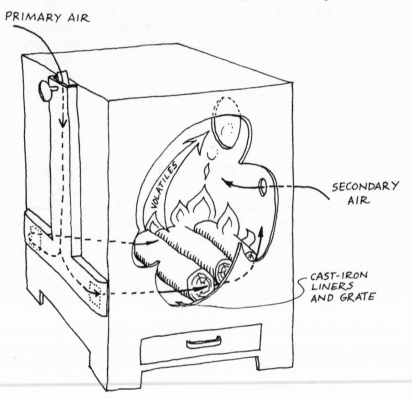

PRIMARY AIR

VOLATILES

SECONDARY AIR

CAST-IRON LINERS AND GRATE

Figure 14   INNER STOVE OF ASHLEY IMPERIAL

What is of more dubious value is the secondary air port located toward the side of the firebox at about the same level as the flue. Only a small percentage of the unburned volatile gases will come anywhere near this point, and it is unlikely that any gases which have not burned at the firebed would benefit from the introduction of fresh air since their temperatures will have dropped too low for ignition.

This model takes logs up to 24″ in length and will heat somewhat more than the 4 or 5 rooms claimed by the company. We rate it at about 12,000 cubic feet with 12 to 24 hours between loadings. Most of the problems people have had with this stove come from *under-using* it. If you want to heat five well-insulated rooms you would be better off with a smaller stove; the largest stove in the world is no good if it doesn't work right.

As with the smaller Ashley Console model, the Imperial has its "carbon copies." The closest of these is the King, which is made by a different division of the company that makes Ashleys. Another similar model has recently been introduced by Shenandoah, the R76.

The current contender for champion of the thermostatically controlled stoves is the Riteway 2000. Its unsurpassed performance and efficiency is based on two basic design innovations. First, the volatile gases which are distilled from the wood must pass down over the level of the coals in order to make their way out of the stove. This preheats them well above ordinary combustion temperatures. Then, in a special combustion chamber, preheated secondary air is mixed with these gases to give maximum possible combustion of the volatiles. Additionally, the damper on the Riteway stove is equipped with a special magnetic catch which converts the action of the thermostatic regulator to a full-on or full-off cycle. This results in higher temperatures during the combustion cycle thereby further increasing the amount of complete combustion. When the thermostat indicates that enough heat has been generated, the primary air is shut off and the fire starts to quiet down. Distilled volatiles still receive secondary air, and are burned in the gas combustion flue, until the level of distillation subsides. At this point the fire appears to be out. When the thermostat calls for more heat and the primary damper opens again, the sleeping coals spring readily back to life and the fire charges up again. This clean burning of the volatiles not only increases the amount of heat obtained from the wood, but makes the Riteway less prone to develop creosote deposits in a cool chimney. It is significant that the Riteway is the only improved efficiency stove we know of that we have been able to equip with a sizable heat exchanger without having creosote problems result. Although the Riteway 2000

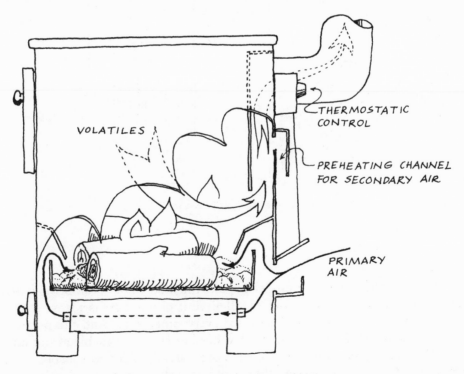

Figure 15   RITEWAY 2000

can heat up to 20,000 cubic feet of insulated living space, the magnetic damper enables it to function just as well and just as efficiently for smaller areas. It can easily go 12 to 24 hours between loadings. By using our densest firewood, hickory, we have kept our 1,300 square foot house at 70° for 42 hours at one loading, with outside temperatures well below freezing. The Riteway 2000 sells for around $300. Optional extras include a water-heating tank and a plenum jacket for converting to a convected-air system.

Riteway has recently re-introduced its model 37 wood and coal burner. Its design and construction are similar to the model 2000, except that it is bigger and features firebrick liners and cast-iron grates and gas combustion flue. As a wood burner, the model 37 has the capacity to heat up to 30,000 cubic feet of insulated living space, which is twice the size of most houses.

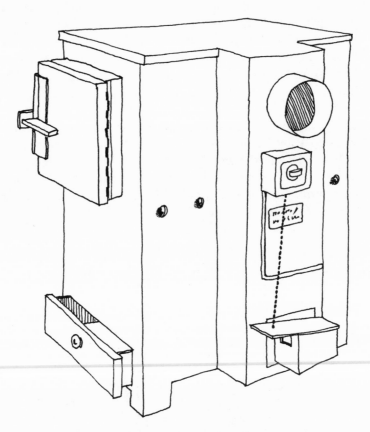

Figure 16   RITEWAY 37

On the other hand, the model 37, like the model 2000, can be operated just as efficiently at less than its full capacity. Believe it or not, here is a stove that for most heating requirements need only be loaded every other day. And the price is around $425. A plenum jacket and two sizes of water heaters are available as options.

The thermostatically controlled stoves are durable, reasonably priced, and marvelously effective. However, their weakest virtue, to many people, is their appearance. Many people consider these stoves to be a little on the homely side, or perhaps just a bit too austere looking. Serious wood stove people will forgive them this and readily bring them into their home, but those who would prefer a more classy-looking stove need not be disappointed. There are aristocratic wood stoves available to all who are willing to pay the price.

The Combi-fires are handsomely styled cast-iron stoves which provide both the romance of an open fire and the efficiency of an airtight stove. Unfortunately they do not do both of these things at once, but what do you expect from aristocracy?

As with modern airtight box stoves, Norway and Denmark have provided the leadership here, with the Jøtul no. 4 and no. 6 and the Morsø 1125.

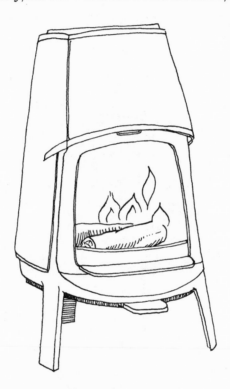

Figure 17   JØTUL 4

The Jøtul 4 is a heavy cast-iron Combi-fire that features a door which retracts beneath the stove when open, firebrick liners, and a very modern styling — definitely the "Scandinavian Look." It takes a 14" log and will burn for 12 to 14 hours on a full load when the door is closed, heating up to 8,825 cubic feet. It is available in a painted black finish for about $650, and in flat green enamel for about $750.

The Danish Morsø 1125 is also of heavy cast-iron construction with extensive use of firebrick for the base and lining. The two doors are side-hinged, and can be easily removed. A full load of 20" logs will burn up to 16 hours, heating 10,000 cubic feet. In the 1125, air is drawn in through the door handle, which keeps the handle cool. This has one drawback since the stove can then only be set at a minimum low setting. Priced around $650, comes in green, black, or white enamel.

The Jøtul 6 is a more dramatic-looking unit with a prominent hood which projects like an emperor's deep meditative brow. The curved doors slide around the cylindrical body of the stove on curved tracks, offering a wider angle from which the fire can be viewed. The liners are of cast iron. Closed, this stove will heat up to 8,000 cubic feet. It takes 14″ to 16″ logs, burning 12 hours at a loading. It is available only in black at around $850.

All of these Combi-fires are surprisingly popular. They are quite versatile in their ability to blend in with their surroundings. They are able to fit in well with either a traditional or modern setting, and will also harmonize quite charmingly in a rustic vacation cabin.

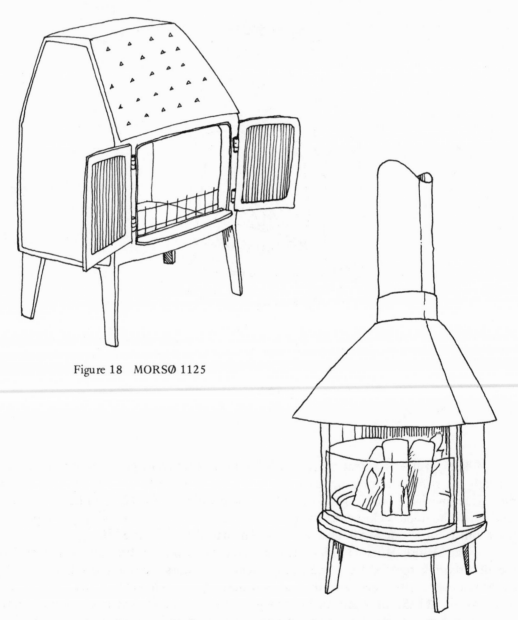

Figure 18   MORSØ 1125

Figure 19   JØTUL 6

A heavy steel Combi-fire, the Gibralter IV, is equipped with a heat-tempered window in the door through which the fire can be viewed. It is a rugged stove without the handsome styling of the cast-iron imports. To some folks it will definitely look just fine. We have no information on this stove's performance, but it should be on a par with the Sierra.

If you are one of those people who yearn for the friendly atmosphere of a glowing fire, yet have a real need to heat economically and efficiently, the Combi-fire is the answer for you.

COOKING WITH WOOD

Interest in woodburning cook stoves has picked up in recent years, but people are not buying them nearly as much as they are buying heating stoves. There are several good reasons for this. For one thing, heating bills have been hitting the pocketbook a lot harder than the cost of cooking fuel. Also, heating stoves do not require as much cutting and handling of wood. People seem more ready to respond to the enjoyable qualities of wood space-heating; cooking with wood can be a lot of fun but it takes a certain type of "vanishing American" to relish getting used to it.

None of this explains why people who are interested are still not buying. The answer seems to be that they are not willing to pay the high price being asked for merchandise of less than exceptional appeal.

Historically, the elaborately ornate cast-iron ranges of great grandmother's day were outmoded by less expensive and smaller "modern" looking porcelain enamel steel ranges. These are currently widely available and range in price from $250 to $500. Currently, the utilitarian styling of these units has become subtly equated with poverty status, at least among many of us rich folks. We would prefer to go back to the old cast-iron stoves but that is out of the question. Not that the old stoves are no longer made, they are. However the prices are now quite high, from $300 for a very small stove to at least $1,000 for one like grandma got rid of. To add insult to injury, the quality of workmanship has declined somewhat from the grand old days of cast iron.

Workmanship is still excellent for many of the imported European ranges, both in cast iron and porcelain enamel steel models. The prices are correspondingly higher.

In all likelihood this situation will be changing in the years to come. As electric utility rates rise and as reserves of natural and L.P. gas are depleted, the cost of these fuels will provide increased incentive for investment in a wood cookstove. As the market grows, manufacturers will be able to pay more attention to updating their products and bringing them into line with the demand.

For the time being, there is nothing wrong with buying one of the currently manufactured models if you seriously want to start cooking with gas (gas from a wood fire). Inflation will probably reduce the difference between what it cost and what it is worth.

Here is a list of major sources of currently available cook stoves:

CAST-IRON RANGES

Atlanta Stove Works, Atlanta, Georgia	small cast-iron ranges at about $300, not the best quality
Portland Stove Foundry, Box 1156, Portland, Maine 04104	small range about $500 Queen Atlantic about $1000 Norwegian Trolla about $500
Kristia Associates, Box 1118, Portland, Maine	Norwegian Jøtul, about $600
Hoskin Diversified Industries, Schoolhouse Farm, Etna, New Hampshire 03750	Austrian Scandia, about $700

PORCELAIN ENAMEL STEEL RANGES

Autocrat Corporation, New Athens, Illinois 62262	Hillcrest and Ridgetop Ranges, from $230 to $300
Preston Distributing Company, Whidden Street, Lowell, Massachusetts 01852	Jet compact range, about $400
Washington Stove Works, Box 687, Everett, Washington 98201	Olympic Wood, Oil, and Marine Ranges, about $300 to $500
Enheat Limited, Fawcett Division, Sackville, New Brunswick, Canada	Fawcett Compact Ranges
The Merry Music Box, 10 McKown Street, Boothbay Harbor, Maine 04538	Austrian Styria Ranges, about $1000 to $2000
Scandinavian Stores, Incorporated, Box 72, Alstead, New Hampshire 03602	Swiss Tiba cookstoves, wood, wood–electric, wood-gas

ALL PURPOSE STOVES

From time to time, certain "smart Alec's" will try and disturb our pleasant reveries by assuring us that hidden in the depths of our being there is a capacity to accomplish anything. History usually refers to such people as "enlightened visionaries." We can usually be counted on to do everything we can to demonstrate the uselessness of their ideas, especially when such crackpots are in our immediate vicinity.

The stoves we are now going to discuss are an outward visible manifestation of this inner search for perfection. Useless as the ideas which give birth to such stoves may be regarded, the material result is somewhat impressive.

First we shall explain what must be the ultimate barrel stove. This combination space heater-and-cookstove was originally invented and built by Ken Kern for his own use. After reading about it, we sent some suggestions on possible modifications and were very surprised to receive an enthusiastic letter from Ken saying he intended to sell the first stove and build another one using our modifications. Now this in itself is an excellent example of the carefree disregard inventor Kern has for the normal rules. The rule is, for those who have forgotten, that when someone gives you a good idea, to act as if you had never heard it, filing it away in the back of your brain for future "discovery" when you will take all the credit for it.

At any rate, here is an illustration of how the stove works: the chief features of the stove are the use of a 35 gallon oil drum set inside, and welded to, a 55 gallon oil drum outer shell. The use of oil drums was chosen because of their availability, their low cost, and their strong curvilinear construction. The cooking surface is a sheet of 1/4″ steel plate welded to the top of the intersecting drums. Interior baffles of salvaged cast iron, or thick steel plate, are held in place against the sides and back of the stove by being firmly imbedded in the refractory cement base. The primary draft is admitted at the back of the firebox through two 2″ iron pipes and is regulated by a thermostatically controlled damper on the back of the stove.

During cold weather a squirrel-cage fan (virtually silent) mounted beneath the outer drum is used to help circulate the jacketed hot air into the room.

A second 55 gallon drum encases the oven at a convenient level above the cooking surface of the lower level drum. Hot air flows from the bottom outer drum through a 3″ stovepipe through the central chamber of the upper-level drum, which acts as a heat exchanger, and from there out into the room or to wherever it can be ducted.

A section of heavy steel well-casing, or a cast-iron sewer pipe, can be used for the gas combustion flue. A 1″ iron pipe allows secondary combustion air to be drawn directly into this combustion chamber. A coil of 1/2″ soft copper tubing wrapped around the gas combustion flue is used for domestic water heating and, as a side effect, reduces excess temperatures above the cooking surface.

Water heating is only one of numerous functions of this stove design. As shown in figure 20, by adjusting a damper, a blower switch, or a baffle plate, one can use the stove for direct or remote room heating — or one can cook, bake, dehydrate, smoke food, or heat water.

Complete plans for the construction of the original stove are included in supplement 19/1 of the Owner Built Homestead. We have paraphrased Ken's instructions in appendix III and included our added innovations.

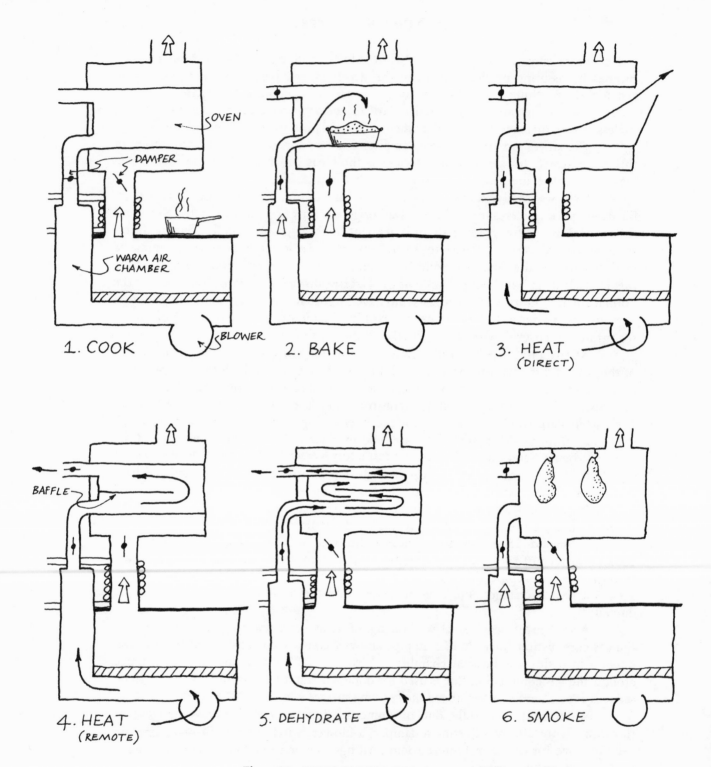

Figure 20   KERN BARREL STOVE FUNCTIONS

If Ken Kern's super barrel stove is a do-it-yourselfer's dream come true, the Defiant parlor stove promises to be the ideal ready-made stove. It is being developed by Duncan Syme in central Vermont. Its design was inspired by the architectural history of that area and can be described as Federal period, which dates from the early 19th century.

Figure 21   DEFIANT PARLOR STOVE

Like the European Combi-fires, the stove is a cast-iron airtight type that can be opened for viewing the fire. Like the Riteway, it is equipped with a thermostatically controlled damper and secondary gas combustion chamber where volatiles combine with preheated air. Additionally, it can be converted for cookstove function at the flip of a lever. It takes logs up to 26″ long and can hold a fire for 14 hours.

Since this stove is so newly developed, and especially since a request for a model to be tested at the Williams College Center For Environmental Studies has been refused, we are not able to comment on this stove's performance. From what we know of stoves, it should be very effective functionally, but there is no way to judge the durability of the castings. The small foundry that has been doing the casting has been having the usual share of difficulties, and production may be behind schedule. The stove is currently priced around $550.

USING A FIREPLACE FOR HEATING

If you are fortunate enough to have a fireplace located fully inside the house, the addition of glass or steel doors can greatly add to its heating capacity, effectively converting the fireplace into a stove.

It is becoming much better understood that the average fireplace is not a very good heater. There have been very few accurate studies made, but Professor Jay Shelton at the Williams College Center For Environmental Studies tells us that the only conclusive studies he has come across indicate a net efficiency of zero.

How can this be? How can you burn a fire and not get heat? The reason is the heat goes up the chimney. If the damper is open too much, as it almost always is, not only the hot products of combustion go up, but warm air is also drawn from the room. At night, when the fire dies down, warm air continues to rise up the chimney. With no fire burning, the warm air is rising from your heating system going directly to the outside. Believe it or not, many fireplaces can be used to cool down a house!

There are several brands of heat-tempered glass doors which can be easily mounted over the front of a fireplace opening. They are available in many different sizes and styles. Air is let in through a grill at the bottom and can be regulated to provide enough for the fire and no more. The special glass will resist very high temperatures, and the best units have a second air inlet above the doors to allow a slight draft to be drawn down just behind the glass. This serves as an extra precaution against the glass cracking. Another feature of top quality units is that the doors snap out easily for convenience in cleaning. With use the doors will accumulate a light coating of carbon soot. This does not interfere with the heating effect — remember you turn your fireplace into a stove — but if you want to see the fire through the glass, you will have to wash off the carbon film regularly.

Figure 22   FIREPLACE GLASS DOORS

Prices of doors run from $100 to $350, depending on quality, size, and accessories such as drawscreens.

If you can't accept glass in front of fire, you can order heavy steel-plate doors from Sturge's Heat Recovery, Stone Ridge, New York.

You can expect to more than double the heat output of your fireplace by equipping it with doors. This is better than you would do with a heat circulating fireplace. Of course if you have a heat circulating fireplace, you can still add glass doors and improve the efficiency just as much.

But chances are your fireplace is sitting with its tail end sticking out into the elements. What do you do then? Well, you *don't* want to convert it into a stove; that would simply heat up the masonry outside your house. Adding glass doors will still let you shut off excess drafts when the fireplace is not in use, but when burning a fire, they should be left open.

Numerous contraptions have appeared for convecting heat from the fireplace into the room. Some of them work very well, others not so well. The best advice is ask the man who owns one. (Hey, this goes for stoves, too, doesn't it?) We like the New England Fireplace Heater because its stainless steel grate will last much longer and its powerful fan really moves a lot of hot air back into the house. The fan may be a little bit loud for some people.

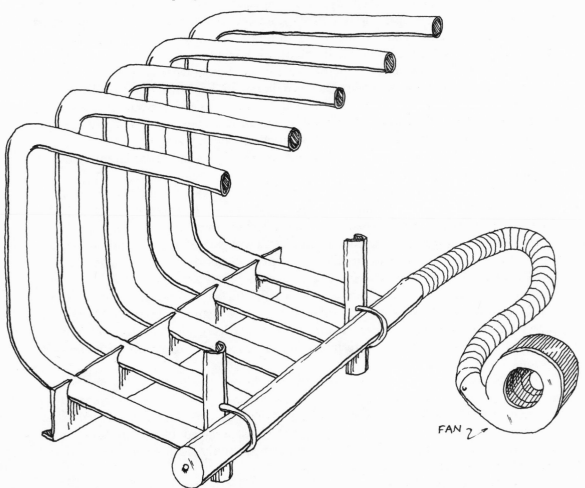

FAN

Figure 23   NEW ENGLAND FIREPLACE HEATER

The Hydrohearth is a similar muffler tube type device used to heat water to be distributed in a hot water heating system. The tubes are not made of stainless steel, but they are not supposed to get hotter than 250° F. because of the water circulation.

One word about air — the fireplace has to draw it from someplace. Stoves do also, for that matter, but a stove uses only 10% of the normal air circulated through a house; a fireplace, if not equipped with doors, will use much more. If air can be inducted directly from outside the house, the fireplace will not be pulling cold drafts under the doors and over the floors. For an average fireplace, two 6″ diameter ducts will be needed. These can be run from a basement or crawl space to a convenient place near the hearth and should be provided with dampers to shut off the air when not in use. For stoves and glass-screened fireplaces a single 4″ duct is adequate.

New Fireplaces

Fireplaces fall into three different structural categories: masonry, metal built-in or "zero clearance" units, and free-standing fireplaces. Heat circulating fireplaces are functional variations of the masonry or built-in types.

The most important property of a fireplace, especially a masonry one, is its permanence. For this reason it is well to do a lot of advance planning before you actually start. Even if you are intending to hire a mason you owe it to yourself to have a well-informed idea of how the fireplace will be built.

We know of no better way for the average homeowner to get a simple yet thorough education in the art of fireplace installation and construction than by making use of the Sunset Book "How to Plan and Build Fireplaces", available from Lane Books, Menlo Park, California. This book discusses just about every conceivable type of fireplace in great detail and has lots of pictures and illustrations.

We will add here just a few comments pertaining to the economical use of fireplaces.

As we mention elsewhere, a masonry fireplace will keep more heat in the house if it is entirely contained within the walls of the house. One exception would be if the masonry of a projecting fireplace were insulated as shown in figure 24.

The addition of glass screens to fireplaces will greatly improve their efficiency, but many of the built-in heat circulating fireplace units draw the circulation air directly underneath the firebox, in which case the glass screens would have to be mounted the required distance above the hearth and an additional baffle plate provided to provide combustion air only through the dampers in the screen, while allowing free circulation of room air underneath. At least one manufacturer, Preway, has glass doors which do not interfere with the circulating room air available as an option.

There are a few fireplaces which offer rather unique features deserving special comment. The Jøtul System 15 is a heat circulating type firebox made entirely of cast iron, elaborately adorned with Nordic bas-relief designs. Due to its design, which is similar to the efficient heat-radiating fireplaces designed by Count Rumford, it puts out a respectable amount of heat for its comparatively small size. A raised-hearth installation makes the fireplace appear larger.

The Hydroplace is a heavy gauge steel double-walled water-heating unit. It becomes a built-in component of a typical masonry fireplace. The water is heated as it flows through all parts of the Hydroplace, and distributed to the heating units throughout the house. It can be installed with any type of hot water heating system.

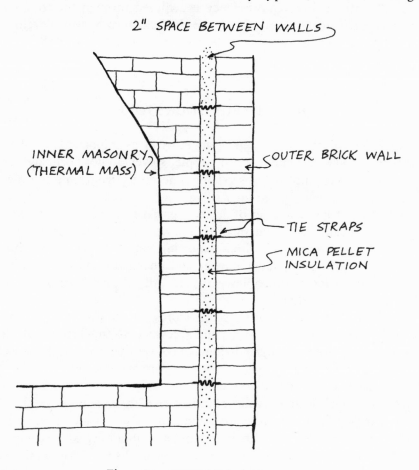

Figure 24   INSULATED FIREPLACE

Both the Hydroplace and the Jøtul System 15 will benefit by the addition of glass screens.

The most popular heat circulating built-in is the Heatilator Brand model 3138C. This is a pre-engineered package so easily installed that 85% of the people who buy them choose to do the job themselves, saving a sizable amount of money. Additionally, the unit itself is one of the most competitively priced on the market. The cost of the basic unit, plus a typical twelve foot pre-fabricated chimney package, comes to a little more than $700.

The circulated hot air can be conveniently carried to any part of the house by using relatively inexpensive double wall ductwork. Fans to increase the rate of circulation are also available.

In one test with a 3138C, the temperature of an otherwise unheated 24' x 30' room was kept constant at 70º F. The outside temperature was 29º F. and the fire was fed 22 lbs. of wood every hour. (That works out to a heating capacity of 1,800

BTU's per lb. per hour, or an efficiency of over 25%.) The model 3138C will soon be available with tempered-glass screens, which should further increase this efficiency.

The ultimate in fireplace efficiency is achieved through the total combustion-maximum heat exchange engineering of the thriftchanger system, developed by Paul Sturges. His hybrid masonry built-in is discussed at length in chapter 5.

WHERE TO BUY YOUR STOVE

The choice of where you buy your stove is as important as what stove you choose to buy. Unlike automobiles and people, stoves do not normally need periodic check-ups, but like other appliances, servicing is necessary from time to time, especially if you find a defect in some part of your stove.

Many more shapes and sizes of dealerships have sprung up than there are makes of stoves. These include large and small established retail chains, lumber yards, hardware stores, general stores, gift shops, sporting goods stores, craft shops, related businesses (steel yards, glass, lawn mower and chain saw sales), and oil companies (yes! but only small local companies, so far). All of these mentioned so far have often added stoves as a sideline.

Then there are the exclusive stove stores which vary from huge "fireplace shops" carrying every conceivable stove and accessory, to small stores which specialize in just one brand of stove. Many individuals take on the stove business as a sideline, selling the stoves out of their homes, as do many farmers, contractors, teachers, policemen, retired people, and people in communes.

Generally, one's dealings will be limited to whomever is geographically closest. If you have a choice, however, here are some important considerations. It is better to buy your stove from someone who is enthusiastic about wood heating, rather than from someone whose primary interest is in merchandising a commodity. Morever, a good stove dealer will be concerned with the quality and reliability of his product and will stand behind what he sells you. Try to determine if a prospective dealer will be *able* to stand behind his product in years to come. All the sincerity in the world is wasted on a poor businessman who cannot afford to stay in the business.

Be especially wary of dealers who consistently discount their prices to make sales. The mark-up in wood stoves is not nearly as much as with most other retail goods. Any dealer who discounts prices and gives servicing such as backing the manufacturer's warrantee will soon be working for very low wages, and may no longer be in business when you really need him. Your best bet will be someone with an established business reputation who is proud of his wood stoves. If a dealer also sells accessories such as insulated chimney packages and stovepipe, so much the better. A dealer who offers installation service is exceptional.

Several stove manufacturers and importers work through "franchised dealerships." While this ensures that the dealer has access to parts, it provides no guarantee that he will be any better qualified to represent the company. Although a few stove manufacturers offer dealer seminars, held annually to give dealers an in-depth acquaintance with their product and the organization that distributes it, a great many "franchised dealers" never attend.

One New England stove importer has built up a very sophisticated system of "exclusive" dealerships, yet allows distributors to place competing dealerships within a few miles of each other. Superficially there is nothing wrong with such contradictions in policy; it is very much in keeping with the system of free enterprise. On a deeper level, however, such practices immediately undermine any commitment a dealer might have to the product. It is possible, though, that this particular importer is aware of such liabilities since we now hear that he would like to set up dealerships "like General Motors."

What about used-stove lots? Seriously, the trade-in business is flourishing in New England. There are dealers who buy stoves with factory defects at distributor's prices, replace the defective part, and sell the stove, virtually brand-new, at a percentage of the retail price. Still other dealers are taking used stoves in good working condition as trade-ins for new. Just as with cars, some stoves have higher depreciation rates than others. We will know that the stove industry has come of age when dealers refer to "blue books" for standard depreciation rates.

To locate the dealer nearest you for a particular stove consult the list of manufacturers and distributors in appendix I, and write for the appropriate information.

Star Windsor for Wood Only.

44098 Has a false bottom and back lining, deep ash pit, double end door. An excellent stove and one that will give satisfaction. Pilasters, panel, urn, rail, etc., nickeled *No* ash pan furnished with this stove. Height of No. 22 and No. 24, without top ornament, 38 and 40 inches; height of ornament, 10 inches.

44098--

No.		Fire box.	Shipping weight.	Price.
22	Direct Draft	22 in.	190 lbs.	$10.25
24	"	24 in.	210 "	11.79
22	Base Heater	22 in.	220 "	13.33
24	" "	24 in.	250 "	14.83
22	Parlor Cook	22 in.	210 "	12.82
24	" "	24 in.	235 "	14.53

Size of oven for the above Parlor Cook.

No.	Length.	Height.	Depth.
22	10 1-2 inches.	8 inches.	12 inches.
24	11 1-2 "	8 3-4 "	13 1-2 "

Star Windsor for Coal.

44099 Large feed door in upper section, heavy iron linings. two covers in top under the swing top, nickeled trimmings. *No* ash pan furnished with this stove. A very durable stove.

No.		Fire box.		Shipping weight.	Price.
22	Direct Draft	14x9	7x9½	210 lbs.	$11.80
24	" "	8x7½	16x10	230 "	13.96
22	Parlor Cook	7x9½	14x9	265 "	14.82
24	" "	8x7½	16x10	285 "	16.53

Size of oven for the above Parlor Cook.

No.	Length.	Height.	Depth.
22	10 1-2 inches.	8 inches.	12 inches.
24	11 1-2 "	8¾ "	13 1-2 "

CHAPTER THREE

INSTALLING AND OPERATING A WOOD STOVE

WHERE TO PUT THE STOVE

Perhaps the best way to get an idea of where a stove should be located is simply to ask yourself where you'd like it to be. Quite often you will think of a place that may be impractical for one or more reasons but it is your house, after all, and you should give good consideration to what feels right to you.

What we shall describe here will be the ideal conditions. You should use them as flexible guides around which your specific plan can develop.

Heating stoves are best located in the central part of the lowest section of a building. The early settlers knew this and usually built their homes around a large central fireplace. Often this was literally the case; the fireplace was built first and then the house was erected, usually by stages as the family grew and "took hold" of the land.

With the advent of central heating systems, fireplaces have been moved to the outside wall in order to give more living space inside the house. Hand in glove with this change has been a shift in function. The fireplace has become more important as a place where the looks and "feel" of a fire can be enjoyed, and less important as a source of heat.

So, we want to bring the source of heat back into the center of the living space. Keep in mind that certain areas of the house such as bedrooms, utility rooms, pantrys, etc., can run cooler. Areas of more sedentary use such as T.V. rooms, living rooms, and bathrooms should be warmer than areas of moderate activity such as kitchens, playrooms, or hallways.

It is a rare house that is designed in such a way as to have a "perfect spot" for a wood stove (see appendix IV: The Weaver House), so some compromises will have to be made. If you have to move the stove out from the center of the house, try to do so along the axis of the ridge of the roof, and slightly off center. This will bring the chimney out near the top of the roof, which is much better. The chimney stays warmer, giving better draft; the house stays warmer and the chimney is supported better with easier access to the top for cleaning or repairs.

If you must put a stove at one end of the house, to take advantage of an existing chimney for example, a metal shield placed next to the wall will reflect a lot of the radiated heat back into the house.

Any small fan directing air past a stove will tend to even out temperatures in the entire house. First try the stove without the fan — it may not be necessary.

In many respects a basement is an ideal location for a wood stove. Since hot air rises, a layer of warm air should develop along the ceiling of the basement.

Excellent control over where the heat goes can be maintained by sizing floor grills to correspond to the amount of heat wanted in a particular area.

If the basement is uninsulated, or if you do not want to heat it, a plenum and and duct system can be built such as shown in figure 25.

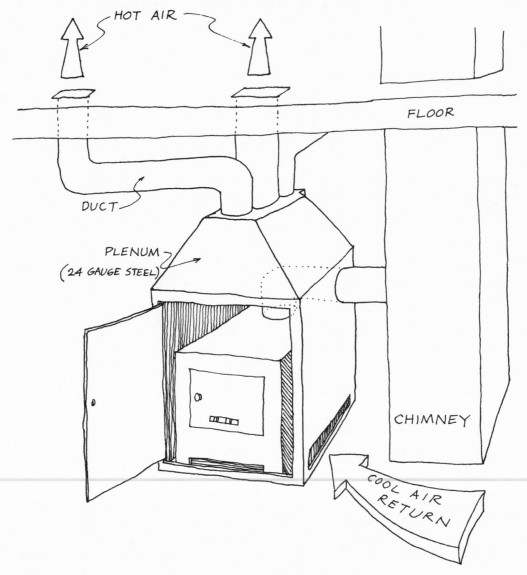

Figure 25 PLENUM AND DUCT SYSTEM

At least one stove manufacturer, the Riteway Company, makes a versatile plenum jacket to be used with either of its two space heating stoves.

This is a gravity flow central hot air system, a simpler and less expensive version of forced air systems now in common use with oil furnaces. If you do not feel like making this a do-it-yourself project, call a local contractor for an estimate.

A simple system of cabinet, ducts, grills, etc., should cost around $400 fully installed. This does not include the stove or chimney.

Location of the stove at the lowest part of the house affords the greatest chimney height, which insures the best possible draft. With the proper stove, this would also be ideally suited to the addition of a heat exchanger. Using a really good heat exchanger is like installing a second stove which uses the flue gases of the first stove as its fuel. More will be said about these unique devices in chapter 5.

THE CHIMNEY

Chimneys do not come with the stoves. Everybody knows this, but not many of us realize how important the chimney is. It is really an integral part of any wood stove. For a stove to perform well under all the various conditions apt to occur during a typical heating season, it is essential that it be correctly hooked up to a good chimney.

The most serious mistake we can make in our attitude toward a chimney is to regard it simply as a means of conducting waste gases out of the house. This might be true of a plumbing vent, but a wood stove chimney is a little more complicated.

The gases leaving a wood stove or a fireplace can vary from 100° F. or less to 1,600° F. or more. Such high and low extremes, however, are rarely encountered. Normally, when used for residential space heating, most stoves operate with a stack temperature ranging from 200° to 700° F. The products of combustion being exhausted at these temperatures consist of water vapor, carbon dioxide, carbon monoxide, and finely suspended liquid tars and acids, usually referred to as creosote for want of a more accurate name.

An ideal chimney would prevent these gases from losing any of the temperature at which they enter the bottom of the chimney until they reach the top. There are two basic reasons for this. The first is to give the best possible draft. As gases cool, they also condense and become heavier. If this happens in a chimney, the gases have to work harder to lift themselves up. This creates a back-pressure effect which restricts the amount of fresh air that would otherwise be available to the fire, even though the intake damper on the stove may be fully open. This, in turn, results in lower combustion temperatures, and a less efficient fire.

The second reason for maintaining flue temperatures is to keep deposits of creosote at a minimum. As temperatures fall below 250° F., many of the suspended tars and acids condense. This mixture, known as pyroligneous acid, runs back down the walls of the chimney or stovepipe and as the water re-evaporates the solid residue is left as a coating on the wall of the pipe. This deposit is what we commonly refer to as creosote. It is flammable but has a comparatively high ignition temperature. Usually it builds up until the accumulation greatly restricts the draft and must be cleaned out. Otherwise it may happen to ignite, in which case it cleans itself out and sometimes cleans out the owner of the house; that is to say the fire may spread out of the chimney and burn the house down. Such calamities are easily avoided, however, by periodically cleaning out the chimney as will be explained shortly. This is a very simple thing to do and does not even have to be done very often if the chimney is built correctly in the first place. Cleaning the chimney once during a season is usually enough to prevent excess buildup of creosote.

Every winter the newspapers carry stories of houses catching fire from wood-stoves. More careful investigation reveals that in a great majority of the cases the fires have not occurred from the woodstoves at all but from their being connected to poor chimneys, connected improperly to decent chimneys, or not connected to chimneys at all.

The most common mistake is running an uninsulated stovepipe out of a window or through a wall and up along the side of the building. The cold air outside the building immediately chills the gases in an uninsulated pipe right at the point where it leaves the building. This eventually results in the rusting out of the pipe and a build-up of creosote where the pipe goes through the wall. It is then very easy for a creosote fire to ignite the wall of the building. This danger can be minimized by periodic inspecting, cleaning and replacing critical sections of the pipe but basically the use of this type of chimney is what we call "asking for it." The owner may have to leave the house and the stove in the care of someone not quite as vigilant. In addition, this type of stovepipe chimney is almost always in violation of local building codes.

An improvement over the simple stovepipe chimney would be to wrap the outside pipe with fiberglass building insulation and cover this with a larger size galvanized pipe, sealing it tightly at the top and elsewhere to prevent water getting in. To keep the fiberglass from melting under high temperatures you can wrap asbestos paper around the inner pipe before putting on the fiberglass.

A drawback to this type of chimney is that while the materials are relatively inexpensive, the job is time consuming and not very permanent due to the fact that the inner stovepipe will need to be replaced within a few years. If your finances are really that short, and you can't wait to get your stove hooked up, this would be an acceptable way to get by temporarily until you can afford a decent chimney. Be sure, however, that when you go through the outside wall, you use a section of double-wall insulated stainless steel chimney.

There has been a tremendous increase in popularity of the prefabricated stainless steel chimneys. Two of the most popular brands are Metalbestos, manufactured by Wallace Murray, Box 137, Belmont, California, and Metalvent, manufactured by Hart & Cooley, Box 903A, Holland, Michigan. These chimneys are approved by the Underwriters Laboratories when properly installed with a 2" clearance from combustible materials. They provide great flexibility in adapting to existing buildings. They can be supported at the ceiling and taken up through an attic or upstairs room, anchored directly to the roof and suspended down into a room from above, or supported by a wall bracket and led out through an outside wall. This latter method is not as satisfactory as the first two because it is more expensive by about $80; there are also more bends in the chimney and, since there is some heat loss through these chimneys, exposing any great length to cold outside air results in an undesirable temperature drop inside the stack.

The cost of materials for those chimneys is rather high — about $12 a lineal foot on the average, but they can be installed by anyone who is reasonably handy with tools. Detailed instructions come with the chimney components and a complete step-by-step guide for the do-it-yourselfer is given in the appendix.

These chimneys can be offset to avoid obstacles, but it is better not to do too much of this if it can be avoided. For one thing, the 15° angle offsets cost about $40 a pair. The appearance of the stainless steel pipe is acceptable to some people; others would want to box in where the chimney goes through an upper room. Such boxing should be removable to allow access to the pipes. Where the pipes go through uninsulated attics it is a good idea to wrap extra fiberglass insulation around them to keep the stack temperatures up.

Perhaps the best type of chimney you can use is a masonry chimney with a ceramic flue tile liner. Masons usually have their own way of building such chimneys. While almost always quite sound structurally, mason-built chimneys are not always made in such a way as to give the best performance. We have made special recommendations in appendix II to be used in building one's own chimney. (It's hard work but most people can do a good job if they are careful.) You can also show this appendix to your mason and come to an agreement with him, before you order any materials, on just how the chimney is to be done. We have mentioned that for keeping heat in your house it is best to have the chimney located inside. If for some reason you must locate the chimney outside, it will be warmer on a south wall. Try to avoid locating a chimney on a cold north wall at all costs. The key to improved chimney construction is to keep it from losing too much heat, as we have said. If you must build an outside chimney on a north wall be sure you have lots of room to surround the ceramic tile liner with fiberglass building insulation. It would be best to build a larger chimney to allow more room between the tile and the surrounding masonry.

If more than one appliance is to be connected to the same chimney, there should be a separate flue for each appliance. This is the general rule. Very often two or more units can share the same flue if they enter at different levels and if the flue is large enough. For example, if you have a stove in the basement with a 6" stovepipe and a free-standing unit upstairs with an 8" pipe, they could both be vented in a flue 10" in diameter. This is the formula for working this out:

$$A = \pi r^2$$

Area equals pi (3.1415) times the radius squared.
Area of 6" pipe = 3.1415x3x3 = 28.2735 sq. in.
Area of 8" pipe = 3.1415x4x4 = 50.2640 sq. in.
combined areas of 6" and 8" pipes: 78.5375 sq. in.
78.5375 divided by 3.1415 = 25 in.
Square root of 25 = 5
2"x5" = 10"
Diameter of chimney = 10".

This formula will work for any number of stovepipes, but there is one thing to look out for. We are dealing here with cylindrical pipe calculations whereas most chimneys are built with rectangular flue tiles. The figures do not transfer from one to the other. This is because there is a difference in the way gases behave in the different tiles. As a rule, flue gases spiral as they rise up a chimney. The sharp corners in a rectangular pipe resist this spiraling motion and impart a drag on the gases. Consequently a rectangular tile must be sized larger than a round one. For example, a 6" round flue will serve where an 8" square flue would be needed; an 8" flue will serve where a 12" square would be needed; and so on.

Masons and masonry suppliers prefer to work with rectangular tiles because they will not roll off trucks and scaffolds as easily as round tiles. Round tiles can be obtained if they are ordered in advance, however, and they are much better functionally than the rectangular tiles.

If two or more flues are being run in the same chimney try and keep the flue to be used for the most creosote-prone stove absolutely straight. Usually it will be the more efficient and slowly burning stove which will tend to develop most creosote. Therefore, instead of slanting a basement flue around a fireplace, you would want to slant the fireplace flue over till it was next to the basement flue.

To prevent pyroligneous acid from seeping through the flue tiles be sure they are well mortared where joined. If you have left an insulation space between the flue and the surrounding masonry there will not be any harm in some leakage, it will tend to self-seal and will not present any exceptional fire hazard. Another reason for being certain that the chimney is tightly sealed is to ensure that it draws well. This may be best understood by making a small pinhole near the top of a drinking straw and observing what it is like to try and draw up liquid through the straw when the hole is letting in air.

The least expensive chimney is the one that is already there. Whether it is suitable for a new stove is something that must be investigated. An unlined chimney, or one whose lining is badly cracked can be quickly ruled out unless the chimney can be repaired or a new lining installed as shown in figure 26. Retrofitting a metal lining is an easy job if you have a straight run and ample room. Lacking either of these transforms the task into a real test of a mechanic's skill. Lacking both, it is best to start looking to alternatives such as tearing down the chimney and beginning from scratch. If you are lining an exterior chimney it is best to fill the space between the liner and the old masonry with loose insulation such as mica pellets. Be sure that the insulation product does not contain styrofoam which melts.

If your chimney lining project is an ambitious one you might want to have a sheet metal shop make your pipe sections out of slightly heavier gauge stainless steel. This would forestall the need to replace the liner for twenty years or so, and is well worth the extra cost of the pipe.

How about connecting a wood stove into the same chimney as the oil burner? Strictly speaking it is against the rules of proper installation for both the wood stove and the oil burner. About half a dozen people have tried this that we know of. Only one has had a problem, and that was most likely due to the chimney being too short. The best thing to do if you are contemplating such a dual use of your chimney is to get a heating technician to check your draft beforehand. If you have a draft measurement of .06″ or better of water, you can most likely hook on the stove — although it will still remain to be seen just how well it will work.

Connecting to a fireplace chimney is another frequently employed tactic. So long as the stove connection comes in above the damper this will work fine.

Many people prefer to set a stove right on the hearth and run the stovepipe back into the fireplace and up to the damper. This works fine so long as the stovepipe clears the top of the fireplace opening.

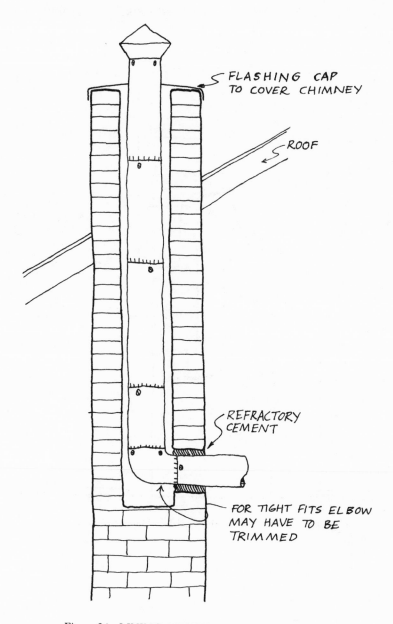

Figure 26   LINING AN EXISTING CHIMNEY

To prevent warm room air escaping up the chimney, some sort of a metal shield should be made. This can be installed inside the fireplace, just below the damper assembly (figure 27) or across the front of the fireplace (figure 28). The latter method, although a bit more involved and not too good-looking, does have the advantage of reflecting heat from the stove back in to the room.

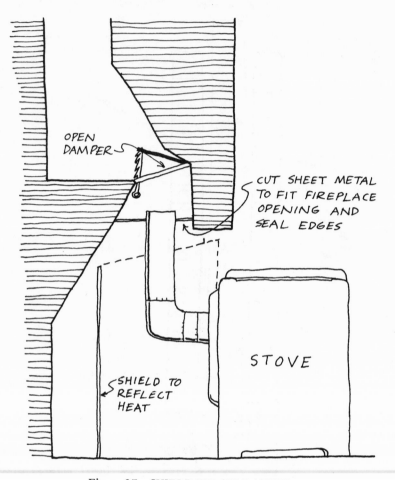

OPEN DAMPER

CUT SHEET METAL TO FIT FIREPLACE OPENING AND SEAL EDGES

STOVE

SHIELD TO REFLECT HEAT

Figure 27   SHIELD BELOW DAMPER

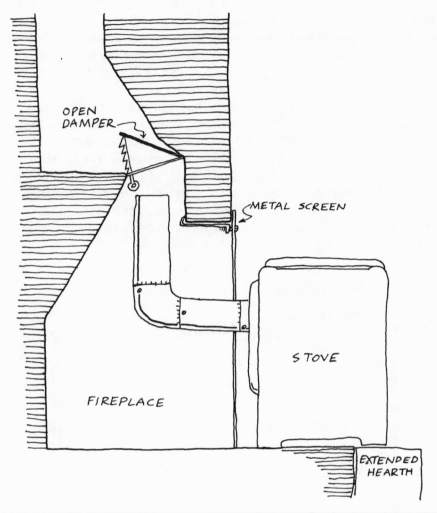

Figure 28   SHIELD ACROSS FRONT OF FIREPLACE

INSTALLATION

When connecting a stove to an existing chimney it is pretty evident where the stove should be located — usually in the closest available spot sufficiently distant from any combustible surfaces. Check your local or state building code for recommended distances. Equally important is to leave some space, at least a few inches, between any part of the stove that gets really hot and a *non-combustible* surface. If you are installing a new chimney, presumably you will decide just where both stove and chimney will be located beforehand.

After you know its exact location, but before setting the stove in place, provisions should be made for the hearth or surrounding brickwork. In tight spots, two layers of 1/4" asbestos board can be mounted on adjacent walls with a freely circulating air space left between them. Asbestos-veneer brick or stone can be added for a handsome appearance, or a stucco effect can be obtained by troweling on a coat of asbestos mastic, available in a variety of shades of grey, including black and white.

Asbestos is non-flammable material but will conduct heat fairly well. This is why it is important to leave an air space. The same thing would apply to stonework or masonry if temperatures were to be hot enough. We have heard of wooden studs igniting from direct contact with heat conducted through sixteen inches of masonry!

Any non-flammable material which will also protect the floor from falling embers, pieces of wood, etc., is suitable for a hearth. Choices range from a thin sheet of metal to fancy ceramic tiles. Quarried stone, such as Pennsylvania bluestone, is a favorite where available. At least one company manufactures light weight masonry-

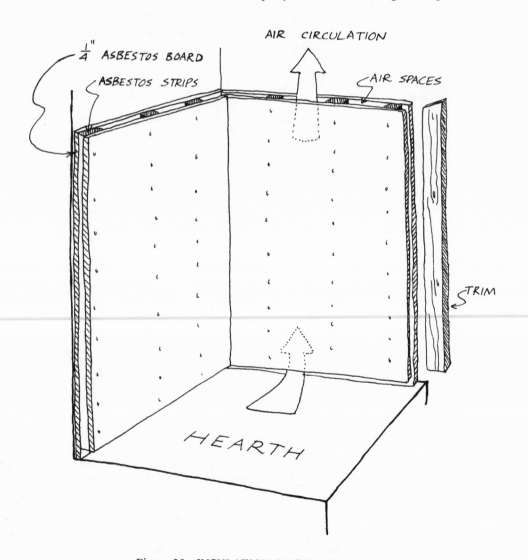

Figure 29   INSULATION OF STOVE LOCATION

type panels to be used as hearths, and protective shields for walls. For further information write: Frank Raferty Distributors, Inc., Box H, Belfast, Maine 04915.

If your hearth is a porous material such as stone or brick, a coat of polyurethane varnish or sealer will prevent staining from ashes or creosote leaks, and it will be very easy to keep the hearth clean and new-looking.

Once the hearth is down, the stove can be set in place and you are ready to hook up the stovepipe.

In selecting stovepipe there are several types to choose from. Light gauge galvanized pipe (28 ga. or 26 ga.) is the most commonly available, but some people have reported headaches occurring when they used this pipe. Galvanized steel will give off toxic fumes at high temperatures, and for this reason we do not recommend its use indoors. Blued steel pipe, similar to the galvanized in gauge and price, is suitable for most installations. For elbows, try to locate the corrugated 90° kind, as the adjustable ones tend to leak.

In some places you will find heavy gauge welded-steel pipe available. This is a better pipe but it costs more than twice as much as the light gauge pipe. It is questionable whether it will last longer enough to be worth the extra cost. You may want to spend the additional money for its good looks; it is usually painted with a heat-resistant paint.

Once you have decided on the pipe you are going to use, get enough sections to hook up the stove. It is better to have an extra section than to be one short. Unused pipe can always be returned. If your chimney flue is larger than your stovepipe size, be sure you get the necessary reducing fitting.

The stove should be connected with short, direct runs of pipe, with a minimum of extra bends, especially if you are hooking up a modern airtight stove. Always install stovepipe with the crimped end down or towards the stove. This will keep any condensation running inside the pipe. Contrary to "logic" this method does not allow smoke to escape under proper operating conditions (adequate draft).

Where lateral runs of pipe are joined you may apply stove putty or furnace cement to the lower portion of the uncrimped section and, after fitting to the crimped end of the other section, reach inside and pack the putty well, leaving a smooth sur-

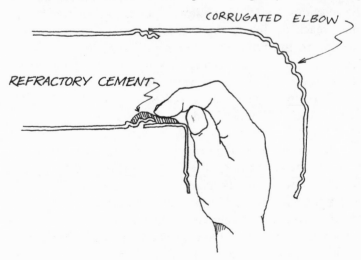

Figure 30   SEALING STOVEPIPE JOINTS

face (see figure 30). Generally it is best to get all your pipe cut to length first, then assemble, working from the chimney back towards the stove, furnace cementing as you go.

When the stove pipe is all joined and cemented, secure all pipe joints with 3/8" or 1/2" no. 8 self-tapping sheet metal screws, 3 per joint. On lateral runs be sure you do not position the screw directly underneath as that will allow leaking (see figure 31).

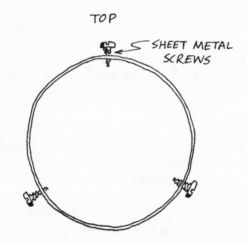

Figure 31 LOCATION OF SCREWS IN PIPE

If you are using a prefabricated metal chimney you will need to have the inner wall of the bottom section crimped with a hand-crimping tool in order to allow the stovepipe to slip up outside it. Normally the manufacturers of such products expect stovepipe to be installed "crimped end up" but this method allows creosote leakage. After slipping the uncrimped end of the stovepipe up over the crimped inner pipe of the metal chimney, reach up inside the stovepipe and be sure the fit is good before securing the stovepipe to the finishing collar with sheet metal screws (see figure 32). Allow several hours for the furnace cement to dry before firing the stove. We have found the following products to be superior to furnace cement for use with stoves and stovepipes: Silver Seal, Industrial Gasket and Shim Co., Box 368, Meadow Lands, Pennsylvania, 15347; Do-All, Wonder Products, Mt. Vernon, New York, 10550.

Once the stovepipe is connected and the furnace cement has cured, you may follow the instructions of the manufacturer or distributor for operation. Be sure you have placed a layer of sand or ashes on the firebed if it is called for. Then start with a small fire and break the stove in gently, gradually adding more wood and increasing the size of the fire over a period of several hours. Do not be alarmed if the stove smokes or smells funny at first, it will most likely be due to the oils in the paint burning off — as often happens with new car motors. Don't be alarmed at anything, in fact; most new stove owners usually go through a short period, similar to when a new baby is brought home from the hospital, when they are a little over-reactive.

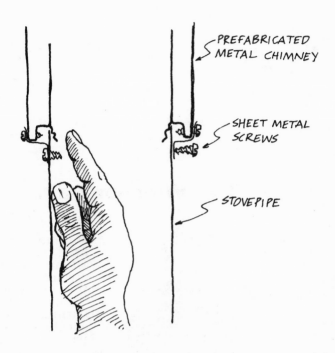

Figure 3 2   FITTING STOVEPIPE TO PREFABRICATED METAL CHIMNEY

Cast-iron stoves require a more gradual breaking-in period — often several days or longer if you are concerned with developing the best possible curing of the iron.

To keep your stove running at top performance, nothing is as important as properly cured firewood. Every once in a while, preferably once a week, you may wish to run an especially hot fire up the stovepipe to scale off and burn any accumulating creosote deposits. This is best done by loosely crumpling a few sheets of newspaper and placing them into the opening from the stove into the flue. Light them and leave the door open a bit to get the best possible draft.

There are chemical products marketed which are supposed to clean creosote but from what we have seen of their use, they sometimes make the situation even worse, creating a hard glassy type of creosote that is difficult to remove. We do not recommend chemical cleaning.

The Windsor Oak.

Our plates are of the very best and our mountings are first class. Special attention has been given to controlling the supply of air to the fire. Our gas burning features are excellent. Our ash pan is twice the size of any other Oak, and it goes in the stove where it belongs. With the best shaking and dumping grate we have confidence in saying we offer you the best Oak in the market.

Height, without top ornament, 42, 45 and 48 in.; height of ornament, 10 inches

For Hard Coal, Soft Coal, Coke or Wood.

		Weight.	Price.
44100	Body 14 in. diameter for wood.	160 lbs.	$11.59
	Body 16 in. diameter for wood.	200 lbs.	13.95
	Body 18 in. diameter for wood	255 lbs.	16.60

CHAPTER FOUR

FIREWOOD

Wood that is freshly cut contains up to 50% of its weight in the form of moisture. The more this wood can be dried out before it is used for fuel, the more its heat value will tend to warm the house instead of going up the chimney in steam.

A minimum of six months' time is necessary to season most wood that has been split and stacked in the open air. A year is better, and a true purist will season the wood outdoors for one year followed by a second year in the woodshed. When really behind schedule, you will still get your wood about 90% seasoned if you have it split and stacked by June, for use the following September. Some woods do not require as much time as others, having a lower moisture content to begin with. Ash, beech, and black locust will be in prime condition after only a few months. Red oak on the other hand needs a full year to season well.

If you do not know how to tell one kind of wood from another, a very helpful book can be obtained free from The American Forestry Association, 1319, Eighteenth St., Washington D.C., 20036, simply by subscribing to a year's worth of American Forests Magazine. The book, "Knowing Your Trees," is well-illustrated with many good photographs showing leaves, types of bark, and general appearance of just about any tree you're likely to encounter.

It is important to stack your wood in such a way that it is easy for it to dry out. Damp places are to be avoided; high on a windy hill would be ideal. Bear in mind that you don't want to trudge too far through the snow drifts to bring the wood to the house. No matter where the wood is stacked, it is important to keep it up on skids, avoiding contact with damp ground. Skids also let you engineer a more or less level base to build the pile upon. Cover open stacks with plastic or roofing paper on top to keep snow and water from entering the stack.

All sorts of charts have been made detailing which woods are heavier, give more BTU's, split more easily, are more decay resistant, etc. As a rule these charts are originally compiled by someone from a Forestry Association or the Department of Agriculture. There are such wide discrepencies between the various charts that rather than try and figure out which one to believe, or add to the confusion by digging up yet another chart, we would like to offer our own observations.

We are very fortunate in having a wide variety of trees growing on our five acre lot, including eighteen hardwood and five softwood species. Over the years we have burned just about everything and we've found that just about everything burns, including the mail and the newspapers.

Generally, wood will give a certain amount of heat per pound, no matter what the species. Since it is all the same to us whether we haul a ton of oak or a ton of aspen, we burn whatever we have at hand.

However, we like to stack separate piles of each species so that we can burn the denser wood during the colder weather and the lighter wood during the milder weather.

We have found that shagbark hickory will really hold a hot bed of coals for an incredibly long time, so we use hickory whenever we are going away for a weekend, or when we want to go a long time between loadings for some other reason.

Another special-purpose wood is white ash. Ash is a reasonably heavy wood that burns quite readily. For this reason we like to use it during mild but chilly weather or on rainy days.

Although our stove will burn whole logs up to 10″ in diameter, we tend to split up our wood as much as possible. The reason for this is that the fire will burn hotter and thus more efficiently, and with less creosote, using smaller splits of wood. The fire burns no faster because the stove is thermostatically controlled. Once we get the needed heat the air supply is shut off. With non-thermostatically controlled stoves the same would hold true but the draft would be choked down manually, or once a year. There is no advantage to splitting wood for an open fireplace because in a fireplace smaller logs do burn faster.

Some wood splits easier than others, we don't pay much attention to which is which, we just naturally tend to do less splitting when the wood is tough. Most wood splits more easily when it is green, and easier still if it is frozen.

Our favorite tools for splitting are a pair of "go-devils" or splitting mauls as they are called by some. Rather than use wedges on big rounds, we prefer to sink a six pound "go-devil" squarely into the center, then drive it down with an eight pound "go-devil." If it gets stuck we use a wedge, but using the little "go-devil" at first avoids bounce-back which can happen with a wedge, particularly when the wood is frozen.

Logs will split most easily along the radial lines which run from the center of the log to the outside. If there is a small crack along these lines, there's where to split the log. It is better to try and avoid splitting difficult pieces of wood such as knotty sections. If you are going to attempt it, split between the knots first, then try halving the sections by splitting through the center of the knots.

If you split logs directly on the ground the "give" of the ground will waste much of the force of your swing. Chopping blocks, on the other hand, often get the wood up too high, especially when you are splitting longer lengths. My solution is to saw off a tree stump close to ground level. Of course, if the ground is frozen hard you can easily split the wood right on the ground.

For cutting your own wood, the chain saw is about the only instrument needed. For most cordwood work, a saw with a 14″ or 16″ bar is ideal. With all the small stuff you'll be cutting, a light saw will be appreciated. There are a lot of good makes on the market; be sure the one you buy can be serviced by a good mechanic, preferably the dealer you buy it from. You can learn a lot from looking at the dealer's service shop. For instance if you notice a large number of saws of a particular make in for repairs you should think twice before buying such a saw.

We haven't had much experience using different brands of saws but it is worthwhile to collect everyone's opinion, and we might as well give ours. Homelite and McCullough are probably the two most popular saws in the country, although loggers and other people "in the woods" will often be found using saws with more foreign-sounding names such as Poulan, Johnsenreds and Lombard. One thing to keep in mind is that such people can often keep a saw's delicate carburetor tuned up better than we can.

We have owned two saws. The first was a small Poulan; it was a good saw but ran out of fuel too quickly to suit us. We traded it in for a Stihl 20 AVP, a saw we are just delighted with. It is very powerful yet light and handy; definitely worth all the extra money it cost. We might not be so pleased if the dealer we bought it from did not have a first-rate mechanic in his shop.

We tried to do our own chain-sharpening but didn't have very much success until an old-timer showed us his method. He first removed the device that fits on the file to show the "city slicker" the correct angle. To file a chain by "eye" simply requires that you watch what you are doing and pay close attention to what you are watching. Do not run the file back and forth as this will dull the file. Bear down only on the push stroke. Three to five strokes should be plenty to touch up a dull chain. If the chain is really in bad shape, or if you've been filing it so much that you are unsure of the angles, take it in to the dealer and have it done on the machine. By filing the chain up near the tip of the bar the chain will not wiggle too much. Advance the chain around the bar by pushing with the file as shown and you will not be likely to get your fingers cut. The hardest thing is to remember where you started filing. Making a mark with the file or a felt tip pen is easier than counting.

After numerous filings, the "drag teeth" between the cutters must be filed down or the chain will just ride on the drag teeth and not cut. A gauge can be bought which will show you when this is necessary. If you have your chain done on the machine from time to time you should not have to file the drag links. If your chain is sharp but you still have trouble cutting, you might check them out.

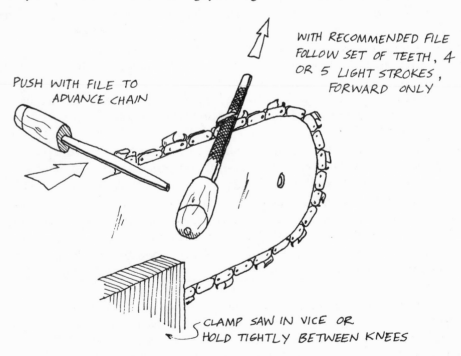

Figure 33   SHARPENING CHAIN SAW

CROSS-SECTION   TANG, FOR INSERTING IN HANDLE

Figure 34   CHAIN SAW FILE

Felling trees is not something one should learn from a book. Learn from someone who has been at it a long time and still has all his good looks and extremities. Chain saws can be dangerous to begin with, and are usually doubly so for the person who has formed less than excellent safety habits, especially when he starts feeling confident. The use of safety goggles is highly recommended since there's no telling when a chip might fly into your eye. The most important safety consideration is always to be well balanced on both feet and aware of any tendency for the tree to suddenly spring back. Don't work too fast.

The one thing we do more carefully than handling a chain saw is buying wood. Not only are wood dealers sometimes less than fully trustworthy, sometimes they just don't know the value of what they are selling.

Usually wood is sold by the cord. A full cord is a stack of wood 4'x4'x8'; a gross volume of 128 cubic feet stacked sufficiently tightly so that about 70% is wood with voids making up the remainder. Wood is also sold by the face cord, the fireplace cord, the stove cord, the pick-up cord, the tier, and so on.

A face cord is a pile 4'x8' by whatever length the wood is cut to. Three face cords of 16" wood and two face cords of 24" wood would each equal one full cord. If a dealer is selling tiers or fireplace cords, or whatever, ask him to explain what these cords are in relation to a full cord. Tell him your definition of a full cord, be sure he understands you and be sure you understand him.

When buying wood you want to find out just what you are getting before you order it. A cord of denser wood such as hickory or oak is worth about $15 more than lighter maple or elm. No one in his right mind should pay money for softwoods such as pine, hemlock, aspen, etc. Neither should you pay for wood before it is delivered, inspected (by you), and stacked. Just because you order a certain type of wood does not mean that that is what will be delivered. You should look over the wood before it is taken off the truck. There's no judging the quantity of wood dumped in a pile so get the wood stacked before you pay. If you have ordered dry wood, and don't know how to recognise dry wood on sight, by all means saw through a piece or two, even split it and try burning it. Some people learn to tell dry wood by knocking two pieces of wood together. Once you get the hang of this you can quickly go on to become a band leader.

Fall and winter are the peak seasons for firewood. Prices will be at a premium for seasoned wood. You can usually buy wood around 30% cheaper in the early spring and let it season for use the following winter. You will also have more choice of what type of wood you can get, how it is cut, split, and you will not be cold if the delivery isn't on time.

At this point we think we'll take back what we said about charts earlier and list some common fuelwoods according to their density and subsequent heating potential in BTU's. Our figures are based on average weights per cubic foot of air-dried wood, as published by the American Forestry Association. With these figures you can quickly determine the comparative dollar value of different species of wood.

SOURCE: "Knowing Your Trees," *American Forestry Association*

AIR DRIED WEIGHT: Per Cubic Foot	Per Cord	TYPE OF WOOD	MILLIONS OF BTU'S PER CORD
53	4505	SHAGBARK AND PIGNUT HICKORY	31.535
52	4420	EASTERN HOPHORNBEAM	30.940
51	4335	MOCKERNUT HICKORY, DOGWOOD	30.345
49	4165	AMERICAN HORNBEAM	29.155
48	4080	WHITE OAK, SWEET BIRCH, BLACK LOCUST	28.560
47	3995	CHESTNUT (ROCK) OAK, BITTERNUT HICKORY	27.965
46	3910	RED OAK, PACIFIC MADRONE	27.370
45	3825	AMERICAN BEECH	26.775
44	3740	SUGAR MAPLE	26.180
43	3655	BLACK OAK, SOUTHERN RED OAK	25.585
42	3570	WHITE ASH	24.995
40	3400	YELLOW BIRCH, CALIFORNIA WHITE OAK	23.800
39	3315	CALIFORNIA LAUREL	23.205
38	3230	RED MAPLE	22.610
37	3145	PAPER BIRCH	22.015
36	3060	BLACK CHERRY	21.420
34	2890	AMERICAN ELM, SYCAMORE	20.230
32	2720	SASSAFRASS	19.040
26	2210	TULIP TREE	15.470
25	2125	QUAKING ASPEN	14.875

Table 2 DENSITY AND HEATING POTENTIAL OF AIR-DRIED WOOD

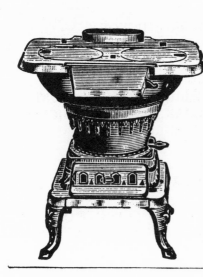

Laundry Stove.

See our special catalogue for other LAUNDRY STOVES.

44110 Laundry Stove for hard or soft coal; has two holes, swing feed door and dumping grate. Made in two sizes only.

No	7	8
Height	24 in.	24 in.
Weight	55 lbs.	75 lbs.
Price	$3.25	$3.55

CHAPTER FIVE

CUSTOM WOOD HEAT SYSTEMS

The recent rise in popularity of wood burning stoves has been truly remarkable and has led, naturally enough, to the next step: the search for a new "Holy Grail" of maximum efficiency.

This movement is still in its infancy however. Most people are more interested in what is "tried and true" and would rather sacrifice the last ounce of efficiency to sleep more peacefully at night. There is much wisdom in the old saying: "The deepest ruts in the road lead to the market." A stove that has been selling well is most likely a good stove, especially if it has been around for more than a few seasons.

But times do change, as we know all too well, and there is often a great advantage to be gained by adapting to something more in tune with the times. Many people are burning the midnight oak trying to figure out how to build a better stove. So far we know of no new contributions, readily available to the market, approaching the effectiveness of such innovations as the bi-metallic thermostat or secondary combustion chamber. This is not so much due to the lack of a developed technology as to manufacturing and marketing limitations. Many small foundries have been severely crippled by new regulations of the Occupational Safety and Health Act and can not afford to develop new products. Some of the larger foundries, such as Atlanta Stove Works, Martin Industries and Washington Stove Works, are a little more able to weather the harrassment of OSHA, but these companies are having no trouble selling the products they currently manufacture so there is not much incentive to venture into something new. This is regretable because the big foundries do have the capacity to make a better product.

The final resort of the intrepid souls who are looking for an improved method of burning wood seems to be in the field of custom heat systems. Just as a car can be tuned up and fitted with high performance carburators and ignition devices, so can the efficiency of a stove be improved.

HEAT EXCHANGERS

The simplest way of improving a wood heat system is to see that a lot of heat is not lost up the chimney. Several very good heat exchangers are available which will rob the stovepipe of its high temperatures and transfer the heat into the living space.

The best of these is the Thriftchanger, developed by Sturges Heat Recovery, Inc. of Stone Ridge, New York. The basic concept of the Thriftchanger is to split up the flue gases so that they flow through numerous small stainless steel tubes. There is a balance point where maximum resistance is developed without throttling the draft too severely. As the tubes are heated by the hot flue gases traveling through them, the heat is conducted to the air surrounding the outside of the tubes. This warmed room air rises through a duct, creating a suction which pulls more air past the hot tubes. This air is warmed, in turn, and a self perpetuating convection cycle results. As the warm air is carried up to the ceiling there are three options. The air can be released at the ceiling, where it would tend to spread out, turning the ceiling into a radiant panel; or it could be carried through the ceiling to warm the room above; finally, it could be ducted to specific locations where heat is wanted. Mr. Sturges calls this a "passive system" because it works by itself without needing a fan to move the air. The Thrift-changer can also be equipped with fans to force air past the tubes. This would be useful for distributing the heat more quickly and thoroughly throughout the living space, but the fans are somewhat noisy.

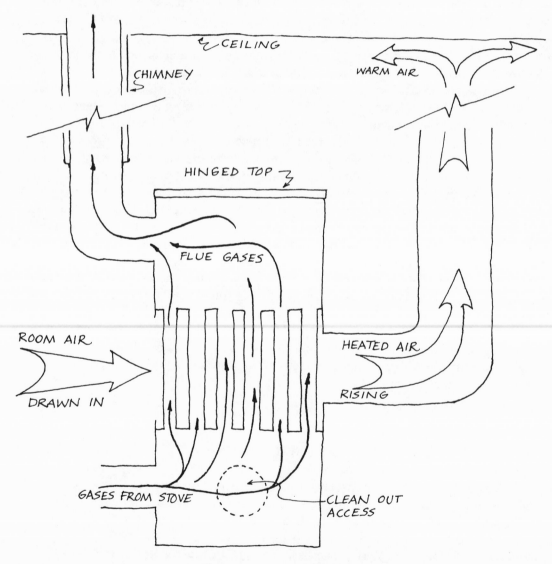

Figure 35   THRIFTCHANGER

From time to time the Thriftchanger requires internal cleaning. This is easily accomplished. The top hinges open for easy access to the tubes and a special brush for cleaning them is provided with each unit. Of all the heat exchangers we have seen, manufactured or homemade, the Thriftchanger is the only one which makes the job of periodic cleaning quick and easy. Each unit is more or less custom tailored to the particular heat system and costs anywhere from $150 to $300. The initial investment should be repaid within the first heating season in reclaimed heat.

Another type of heat exchanger which has become very popular recently due to its comparatively low price and attractive styling, the Magic Heat, manufactured by Calcinator Corporation, Bay City, Michigan 48706, is a smart reproduction of a design that has been around for many years, developed by Torrid Air Manufacturing Company, Inc., of Seattle, Washington. Priced between $65 and $80, the Magic Heat can pay for itself in a matter of months.

In principle, its operation is similar to the Thriftchanger with some roles reversed. The hot flue gases, instead of flowing through the fourteen stainless steel tubes, flow around them. Room air is blown through the inside of the tubes by a thermostatically controlled fan.

The Magic Heat has a built-in cleaning device: a plate with holes cut so that it fits over the tubes, which can be drawn back and forth by means of a rod attached at the center of the plate, extending to a knob in front of the unit. This has several drawbacks. The plastic knob can overheat and melt and the connection between the

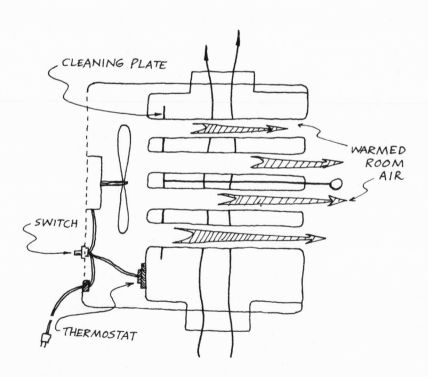

Figure 36 MAGIC HEAT

rod and the cleaning plate can weaken and fail. It will almost invariably do so if there are heavy or unevenly distributed deposits on the pipes. Once the cleaning mechanism fails there is not much that can be done with the unit except to send it back to the manufacturer.

We have found that both the Thriftchanger and the Magic Heat work well on oil burners as well as on woodstoves with low efficiencies, such as Franklin stoves. Many oil company representatives get disturbed at the thought of a heat exchanger upsetting the delicate "adjustment" of the furnace, although they seem to be tolerant enough of anything which would reduce the efficiency of the system. Most any oil man will let you know that if you put a heat exchanger on your oil burner it will immediately acquire the amazing capacity of becoming the cause of every problem which occurs, even if the problems occurred before it was installed! You might want to anchor the heat exchanger to the wall with a short length of chain. If the oil man asks what it is for you can say that you wouldn't dream of leaving a scapegoat in your basement without tying it up.

In all fairness we should say that it is possible to so restrict the draft by the use of a heat exchanger that the performance of the burner is hindered. This is less likely with modern high speed burners. If your burner is this type it will be marked somewhere: 3,450 RPM, and you may use a heat exchanger with impunity. If you have the 1,725 RPM burner it would be best to have a draft test taken by your serviceman. If a reading of at least .06″ of water, negative draft, is obtained you can install a heat exchanger. Such a draft test is also essential for Franklin stoves or free standing fireplaces to insure that smoke will not back up into the room.

The heat exchangers we have discussed so far work on the basic principle of restricting the draft to obtain heat transfer. Because of this, it is important to use them in conjunction with a good chimney. If your draft readings are low you might consider building the chimney higher or installing a draft-inducing fan.

We have not had good results using heat exchangers on any of the low draft stoves such as Ashley, Jøtul, etc. One notable exception is the use of a Thriftchanger on a model 2000 Riteway. We have watched two of these through a heating season and the results have been impressive. With the addition of the Thriftchanger the efficiency of the Riteway has been boosted as high as 78%! This is quite extraordinary. We feel further improvements could be made (see the sketch of a proposed gravity furnace using the Riteway-Thriftchanger combination, figure 35).

There are many heat exchangers which do not work by restricting the draft, and numerous prototypes have been made. The simplest conducts the heat away from the stovepipe using metal fins as in a radiator. This is another passive system which works reasonably well and has the advantage of being inexpensive. A kit containing 16 strips of 30 fins costs about $10. For more information write: Patented Manufacturing Company, Bedford Road, Lincoln, Maine, 01773.

Simpler, and even less expensive, is to simply run a longer length of stovepipe, or put extra bends in it as shown in figure 38. Creosote drips can be a problem with lateral runs of stovepipe. These systems like the draft restrictive types can be problematical when used with air tight stoves.

The use of heat exchangers for pre-heating domestic water is becoming more and more popular, especially with people who have electric water heaters. The use of electricity to heat water is second in inefficiency only to electric space heating. We maintain that electric heat is fine, as long as you don't use it much.

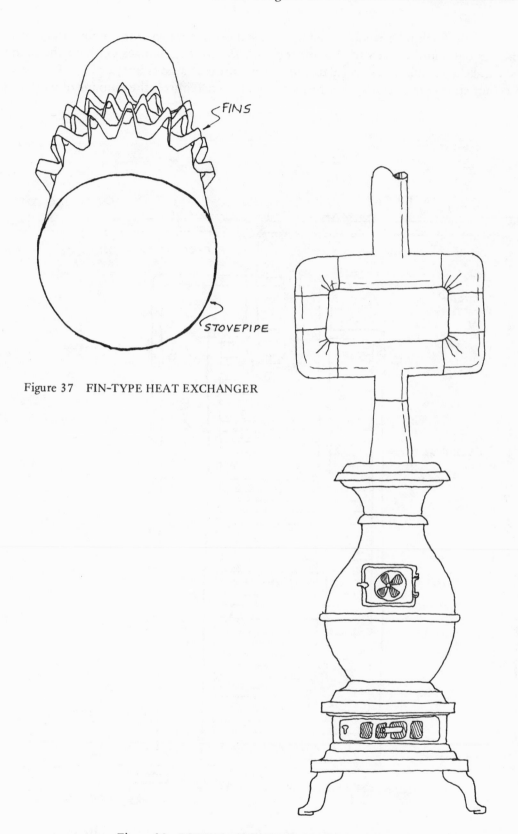

Figure 37   FIN-TYPE HEAT EXCHANGER

Figure 38   POT BELLY STOVE WITH STOVEPIPE HEAT EXCHANGER

By hooking a wood fueled heat exchanger in parallel with a conventional water heater one can do much of the heating with the heat exchanger yet have the thermostatically controlled tank regulate the temperature at a constant setting. The use of a second storage tank is a further refinement which maximizes the amount of work done

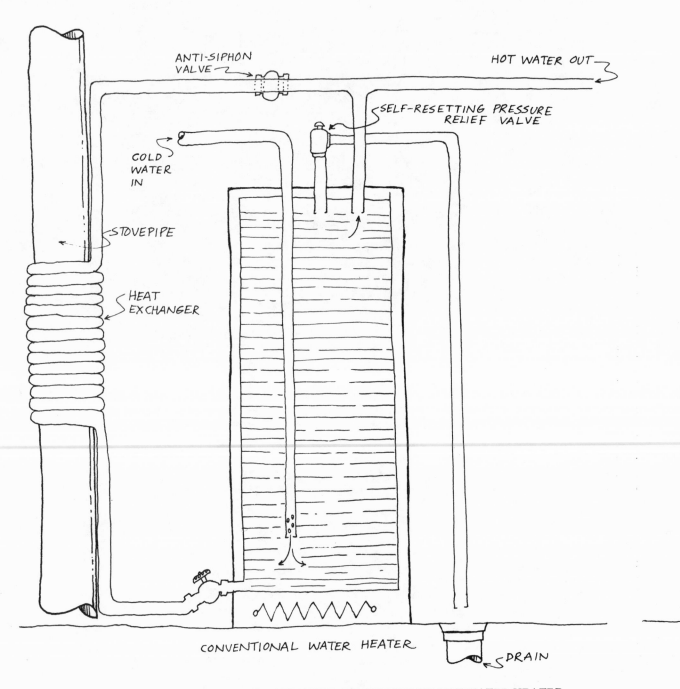

Figure 39   HEAT EXCHANGER CONNECTED TO HOT WATER HEATER

by the heat exchanger. There are several other advantages to the use of a second tank: the larger mass of water has less likelihood of overheating and is excellent insurance against running out of hot water; in addition, an uninsulated tank of hot water will be just about all that is needed for keeping the utility room at a comfortable temperature. If no heat is wanted in the room, simply insulate the tank.

Suitable galvanized steel tanks can be found quite cheaply. If nothing can be found at the local dump look up the surplus metal dealers in the yellow pages of the

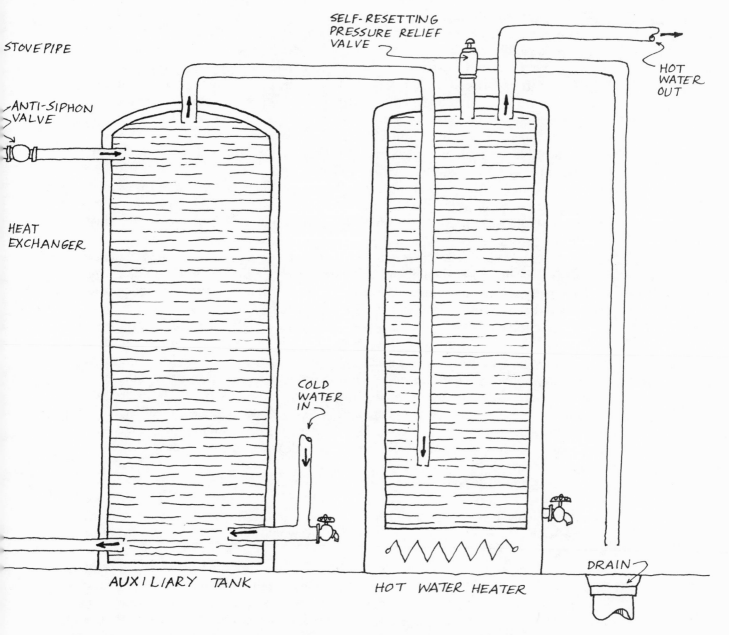

Figure 40   HEAT EXCHANGER AND AUXILIARY TANK CONNECTED TO HOT WATER HEATER

phone book, or try the dump in a neighboring town! Range boilers are available at most any plumbing supply house. They are ideal and not too expensive.

Overheating of the water could be a frequent problem, depending on how well the storage capacity of the tank (or tanks) is matched with the heat output of the heat exchanger. The best provision for overheating is to install self-resetting temperature and pressure relief valves, and to connect them to a suitable drain. As mentioned earlier, the Riteway Manufacturing Company sells water heaters designed to fit inside their smaller wood stoves; these would also fit most rectilinear stoves.

Two very simple heat exchangers for domestic water have been described by Larry Gay in his book, "Heating With Wood." The simplest of these is to run a length of 3/4" copper pipe through the chimney. Larry uses this system himself, in connection with a rather large storage tank elevated upon an extremely stout scaffold and connected in parallel with a small electric water heater. The system works well.

The second type of heat exchanger recommended by Larry Gay involves wrapping a soft copper coil around the outside of a flue pipe. This promises to capture more heat since it can concentrate the transfer of heat at just that point where the flue gases are hottest: the point at which they leave the stove. There is at least one commercial version of such a unit available. It is appropriately named Blazing Showers, and is available with all the necessary attachments for do-it-yourself installation. Information may be obtained by writing to Blazing Showers, Box 327, Point Arena, California, 95468. You might also write to Larry Gay, Marlboro, Vermont to see if he has developed an improved model. We have been pestering him to market something similar to the Blazing Showers, but with a stainless steel inner liner to protect the coils against the corrosive effects of the flue gases.

It seems a shame that most of these ingenious devices for stealing some extra heat from our woodstoves should work more effectively on the less efficient stoves and less effectively on the more efficient models. Fortunately, in trying to understand why this is the case, we have found a way to overcome the limitation.

The problem is that the more efficient stoves are engineered to get most of the heat out of the flue gases before they leave the stove. Further loss of heat, such as would occur in a heat exchanger, usually results in the gases cooling low enough to allow water vapor to condense and form creosote. Creosote deposits on the heat exchanger immediately reduce its ability to conduct heat and soon block up the flue altogether. One answer to this is to burn a hotter fire. As we pointed out earlier, a hot enough fire would burn even the residual volatiles leaving no possibility of any creosote formation, regardless of how low the temperature dropped in the chimney. The only problem with hotter fires is what to do with all the extra heat!

One thing that could be done would be to heat a larger area or, conversely, use a smaller (but hotter) fire in a smaller stove to heat the same area that a larger stove would ordinarily heat. This would have its disadvantages however. More frequent stoking would be required and the smaller stove would have to be able to handle a hotter fire.

The ideal solution might lie in finding a way to store large amounts of periodically generated heat, to be rationed out slowly and evenly as needed. It is very significant that this is the same task that faces designers of solar heated homes, and it is not too surprising that the first major innovation in this respect is occurring in a building designed to be heated by both solar and wood energy.

Professor Richard Hill, of the University of Maine, has developed a furnace which uses venturi-assisted air jets to recirculate combustion gases in a large fire box. When the completely combusted gases leave the fire box they pass through a corrugated steel conduit, such as is used to conduct drainage under a driveway. The conduit runs through a bin of number two crushed stone, transferring practically all of its heat to this storage area.

This system has been designed for periodic, intensely hot, firings to augment the vast bank of solar collectors, also engineered by Professor Hill for the 6,000 sq. ft. office building which is to be the headquarters of the Maine Audubon Society. The building is scheduled for completion in June 1976. More information is included in appendix IV.

Richard Hill's heat system promises to fulfill every condition for total combustion and maximum heat recovery. It is possible that a cleaning problem could occur if combustion is less than 100% complete, which might happen if less than thoroughly dry wood were used. Presumably this will be forseen, and provisions will be made for reasonable access for cleaning in the event it is needed. Professor Hill expects to have conclusive performance results only after a year of testing at normal operation.

The idea of a total combustion or smokeless stove such as this is very intriguing, especially in its implications for conservation of environmental resources. Moreover, Professor Hill's approach is a unique blend of top flight engineering using low cost materials and manufacturing techniques. The Audubon house is a large project, but we don't see why the system couldn't be scaled down to a size more suitable for single family residences.

The concept of "off peak" storage is being developed for a hot water heating system by Mr. Paul Sturges. Although Mr. Sturges and Professor Hill have not yet met each other, they know of each other's work and appear to share similar views on smokeless combustion. Like the Audubon house furnace, Mr. Sturges' system would burn high temperature fires periodically. The heat exchanger would be located in a boiler, however, and the hot water would be stored in large tanks. This system, which is currently in the planning stage, will undoubtedly work well if developed with the same thoroughness as Paul Sturges' many other heat recovery and refrigeration projects.

Mr. Sturges has designed several heat recovery fireplaces which offer the ultimate in top heating efficiency combined with the enjoyable ambience of a visible fire.

These consist of a normal masonry fireplace, of special dimensions, fitted with tempered glass screens and a special Thriftchanger. Additionally there is a damper box by which the Thriftchanger can be bypassed when the glass doors are opened.

In its operation, this system is very similar to Richard Hill's furnace, lacking the "off peak" storage but much more esthetically enjoyable. By the addition of the glass doors, the fireplace is transformed into a virtual kiln, where combustion temperatures are intense even with a small fire. At these high temperatures the Thriftchanger works most efficiently. Accumulation of creosote is almost nonexistent and can be brushed away every few months.

Although this is a very simple system, some details of its development have been very delicate. After years of work, the final refinements were made last winter, and subsequent tests have shown a very high degree of performance. For example, the glass screens, which according to the manufacturer will withstand temperatures of up to 550° with a 6" clearance from the burning wood, have stood up to much higher temperatures (stack temperatures of over 900°), direct contact with flames, and direct contact with vigorously burning wood.

At present, this system requires a custom-made masonry fireplace, but plans are being made to manufacture a pre-fabricated package similar to zero clearance fireplace units. For more information write to Sturges Heat Recovery, Inc., Stone Ridge, New York.

Paul Sturges uses a rather unorthodox approach in that he works from the job site first, before going to the drawing board. Most engineers are trained to do just the opposite and it is quite humorous how several heat recovery projects have been botched up by engineers who have tried to "borrow" Paul's ideas after his initial (and final) consultation.

This is a very important thing to understand. Just because people like Richard Hill and Paul Sturges can engineer fantastic systems like these does not mean that the average mechanic, armed with this book, can go out and improvise, for example, a fireplace heat exchanger for his hot water baseboard heating system, with any assurance that the results will be worth the expense and effort.

Please do not think that we are trying to discourage people from building their own heat systems; we are all in favor of that. It is our contention, however, that a few dollars spent on consulting fees could be the smartest part of your investment.

ARCHITECTURAL INTEGRATION

Whether you are considering a custom heating system or the simplest wood burning stove, careful attention should be paid to the relationship of the heating elements to the rest of the house. We have already mentioned the close relationship that exists between a stove and its chimney, and have pointed out the advisability of locating these in a central part of the house. The reasoning behind these suggestions will become a little clearer as we discuss the relationship between the woodburning appliance and the house in more detail.

The first thing that should be noted is that in most cases the woodburning heater will function as a radiant source of heat. This is in direct contrast to most baseboard or hot air systems, which are primarily convection heaters. Instead of heating the air inside the house, a wood stove radiates heat, like the sun. People or objects are warmed directly by intercepting the path of this radiation. Air is warmed also as it comes in contact both with the stove and with the warm walls and ceiling, but radiation from the stove allows us to feel comfortable at lower air temperatures.

The theory behind this is that for each degree above the mean comfort temperature (68° for most people) provided by a radiant source of heat, the air temperature can be reduced 2°. Thus we will feel comfortable in a room where the air temperature is 66°, providing we are receiving 69° radiant temperature. At 70° radiant temperature the air temperature can be 64°, and so on. This explains why on a cold but sunny day we can be very comfortable outside so long as we are in the direct sunlight and no wind is blowing.

In relating a stove to a house, or as would be appropriate in new construction, in relating a house to the stove, it is well to keep in mind that the stove will be radiating its heat. Thus we would be better off with foil backed insulation in walls and ceilings directly exposed to the stove. This would re-radiate the heat back into the house. We would also want to avoid direct exposure of the stove to large areas of glass, for, just as the sunlight will stream in through thermopane windows and warm the room, so will our wood heat radiate directly out at night and on cloudy days. Covering windows and other glass areas with insulating panels or heavy drapes would permit the stove to be exposed to glass areas and provide an additional advantage: if the room should get too warm, the drapes could be opened and we would be able to cool off. Not only would the stove radiate heat out the window, but our body heat would also radiate out.

This brings to mind an interesting speculation. Human beings have been using central heating systems to keep themselves surrounded by an envelope of warm air when inside for less than a hundred years. For countless centuries before this we have been used to small radiant fires and heavy clothes to keep us warm. It is possible that we have not fully adjusted to our new "constant temperature living." Or perhaps it is more strenuous for our bodies to be constantly adapting to one set of circumstances then another as we go in and out of buildings, cars, etc. Many winter colds and flu spells might be avoided if we lived closer to our evolutionary roots. This theory would be very difficult to prove, of course; we offer it simply as a possible explanation of why many people notice that they feel better once they have gone back to wood heat.

With a radiant heat system we can afford to have more air circulation too. It is essential, in fact, because a stove is constantly pumping air out of the house. This can only happen if more air comes back into the house somehow. In a modern well-built house, the stove will be forced to pull drafts in through such places as windows and doors, unless some provision is made to get fresh outside air to the stove. The Widman House shown in appendix IV was built without any such provision. Fortunately the problem was easily solved by installing vents from the crawl space near the stoves and fireplace. Another solution to this problem would have been to allow more air-flow through the house. A certain amount of air exchange is necessary to keep us supplied with fresh air. A wood stove uses only about 10% of the normal air exchange.

One of the most delightful innovations in adapting wood stoves to the house has been brought to our attention by Ken Kern's book "The Owner Built Home." It is called the "No-Draft Floor Invention," and works like this: since hot air rises, placing the stove over (or under) a grill in the center of the house leading to a crawl space will draw air up from below. Placing smaller grills under windows and doors around the inside perimeter of the house will allow cooled inside air to sink to the basement. This air flow not only keeps the floor free of drafts but tends to dry out the basement and keep the room air normally humid. Insulation of the basement walls would be required to prevent excess heat loss.

If your house does not permit the use of such a passive air circulation system, a lot can be done with a small fan or two. Many people like to install a fan directly in the wall to draw warm air into a cooler room. One clever innovation is to place the fan and outgoing grill at the floor level of the room to be heated, using the space between the studs as a duct and pulling air down from an intake grill at the ceiling level of the room from which the warm air is being drawn (figure 42). The ultimate system of this sort has been employed by a friend of ours who built a special duct into a

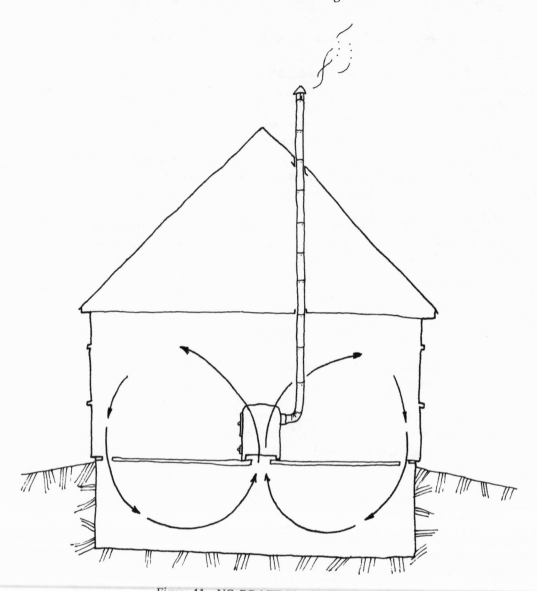

Figure 41   NO-DRAFT FLOOR INVENTION

central chimney of a three story, multi-level house. A thermostat located at the top of the duct activates a small fan, like the type used to cool IBM machines, and the warm air is blown back down to the basement.

There are many other such considerations which will spring to mind only through years of living and working with wood stoves and housing design. The only "crash course" we can think of is "The Owner Built Home." It may be purchased directly from the Author-Publisher, Ken Kern, by sending $7.50 to Ken Kern Drafting, Box 550, Oakhurst, California. 93644. We have learned a great deal from Ken's books and have shared many of our new ideas with him. Similarly we invite people with fresh ideas to write us at Box 158, Glenford, New York. 12433.

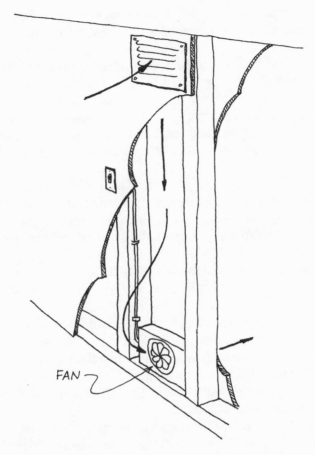

FAN

Figure 42   FAN-IN-WALL CIRCULATING SYSTEM

INTEGRATION WITH SOLAR HEAT AND MULTI-FUEL SYSTEMS

The physical limitations of solar heating design currently permit as much as 84% of the average residential heating requirement to be generated directly from the sun's energy. A more economically practical design would rely on direct solar collection for little more than 50% of the heating load.

In either case a back-up heat system is needed. By this we do not mean a complete conventional heating system, although these are required in projects designed by certain "solar engineering firms," including most government sponsored demonstration projects. The idea is to "cover one's flank" and "not get caught out in the cold."

What we are referring to would be a smaller than usual system designed to produce the 15% to 50% extra heat that will be needed during periods of prolonged cloudy weather. The choices for such systems include: small oil and gas burners, electric heaters (including heat pumps), wood stoves, coal stoves, and fireplaces.

Bruce Anderson, head of Total Environmental Action, and executive editor of "Solar Age" magazine, has described wood heat as the ideal back-up system for solar energy.

In a sense wood heat *is* a solar energy source, having often been called a solar battery. In all fairness this analogy could be extended to coal, oil, and electricity.

The problem with electricity, however, aside from the fact that it is expensive, is that enough solar-electric systems would eventually create a peak demand during times of no sunlight — with virtually no balanced consumption during sunny weather. Also, electric power outages are most likely when the energy is most needed — during winter storms.

Heat pumps run on electricity so they have the same disadvantages, only to a lesser degree, since the amount of electricity needed for a given heating requirement is much less. They are quite popular as auxiliary heaters for solar back-up with people who want a completely automatic system and who are willing to pay a little more for the convenience.

Oil and natural gas are fast becoming fuels of the past. Presumably we should start conserving oil for transportation uses, and gas for cooking and industrial applications.

Reserves of high quality coal, such as would be needed for small heaters, are also on the decline, and the price of coal is climbing as fast as oil.

This leaves wood. Wood requires more handling because of the logs and ashes, but it is relatively inexpensive, environmentally clean, and perpetually self-renewing. A two or three acre woodlot will provide enough fuel for all the cooking and auxiliary heating of a modest solar house.

We visited the Tyrrell Solar House in Bedford, New Hampshire during a February snowstorm. There had been heavily overcast skies for three days previous to our visit. To top everything off, the fancy shading system for the solar collectors was not working, resulting in some extra heat loss. Nevertheless, the only back-up heat needed was provided by the small fires lit in the wood cookstove at mealtimes.

The nicest thing about using combined wood and solar heat is that the technologies for both have similar requirements, permitting the two systems to work in concert. For example, a certain amount of thermal mass is needed for storing heat (tempering extremes of hot and cold). The masonry for an interior fireplace or chimney will automatically add to the thermal mass of the house. Also, the solar-collected heat will help the chimney stay warm, which will insure a good draft.

Figure 43 shows how a centrally located masonry core can be used to duct solar heat down from the roof and up from various wood burning appliances, while serving as a continuous massive but gentle radiator of heat.

The multi-fuel furnace shown in figure 43 represents the ultimate in what we call the "all bases covered" approach to heating. When used in conjunction with an automatically regulated solar heat system, the oil or gas burner would automatically be kicked on when there was no longer sufficient solar heat, either from direct collection or from storage. If the homeowner wanted to conserve oil he could start a wood or coal fire, and the oil burner would go on standby again.

When the fuel crisis reached its first peak in 1973, we were tempted by the vision of buying a multi-fuel furnace, stocking up with several cords of wood, a couple of tons of coal, and a few hundred gallons of oil then thumbing our noses at shortages.

So far we have resisted the temptation. The more we heat with wood the less interested we are in coal or oil. The multi-fuel units become much more practical in multiple residence buildings such as condominiums and apartment houses, where larger units permit correspondingly larger-sized wood to be burned. The combination

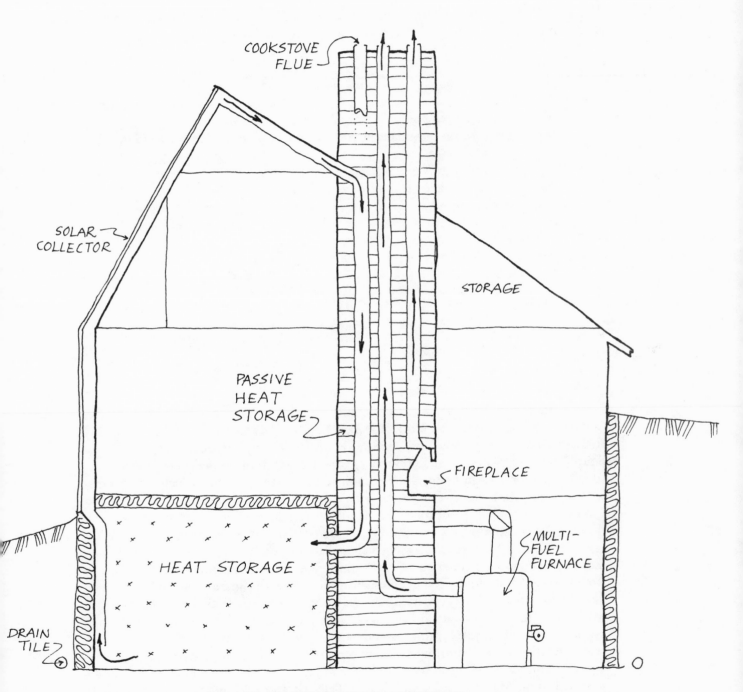

Figure 43   MASONRY CORE HEAT STORAGE

of wood and oil ensures continuous heat under all circumstances. As the resource recovery industry grows, we shall see a new type of fuel, such as recycled paper and cardboard, being produced, which can be easily utilized by multi-fuel burners.

Of course multi-fueled furnaces and boilers do not have to be used in conjunction with solar systems. They can be used as you would a conventional oil burner, or set up simply as a wood or coal burner beside an existing oil burner and connected in series with it.

Of the different brands manufactured we have only seen the Riteway in action. It is everything the company says it is and more. Here is what one customer has to say:

Gentlemen:

As you know, we are enjoying our second winter of use from our Riteway LB-70 boiler which we use to heat our dealership, in conjunction with our old oil-fired boiler that came with the building.

Last winter we saved 4,000 gallons of fuel oil, and this winter it looks like the savings will be even greater. This letter is just to say "thank you" for such a substantial, high-quality product. We have had not a moment's trouble with it, and I suspect we are all in much better physical condition from handling the wood for it than we would be otherwise.

The local countryside is gradually being improved in appearance as a result of our taking the dead trees, and the land-owners all seem to appreciate it. Aside from giving us the wood free, most of them even help us cut and load it on to our truck. Sort of awakens the pioneering spirit for everyone for the Bicentennial year!

> *Yours truly,*
> *John S. Noecker, President*
> *Noecker Buick-Pontiac, Inc.,*
> *Union Turnpike, Rt. 66*
> *Hudson, New York 12534*

Other multi-fuel heaters are manufactured or distributed by: Oneida Heater Company, Inc., Oneida, New York 13421; Marathon Heater Company, Inc., Box 165 R.D. no. 2, Marathon, New York 13803; Duo-Matic, 2413 Bond Street, Park Forest South, Illinois 60466; and Tekton Design Corporation, Conway, Massachusetts 01341. Tekton Design imports the Scandinavian HS Tarm boiler, which burns either wood or oil. Although we have not seen this unit, we have received a favorable accounting of it from Jim Nichols, who handles a very large selection of stoves. He says that the Tarm is made of a very heavy gauge material and is a very good unit for the price. It costs a bit less than an equivalent Riteway boiler. It is doubtful, however, that the woodburning function of the Tarm would be as efficient as the Riteway. It would be an ideal choice for people who want to heat primarily with oil but would like to use wood as a secondary fuel. If wood is to be used as the primary fuel, it would be wise to check out the various heaters rather closely. If possible, see them in action. Remember, these furnaces and boilers are built to last a long time; any increase in efficiency will most likely repay the additional cost within a few years.

Furnaces which burn wood only are made by Waldo G. Cummings, Fall Road, East Lebanon, Maine 04027 and Perley Bell, Grafton, Vermont. Mr. Cummings' furnace was still in the prototype stage last spring (1976), but coming along nicely with impressive results from the working model. We like the fact that Mr. Cummings chooses to use cold-rolled steel which, though harder to work with, will hold up better under high temperatures. Most impressive is the price, which is expected to be under $1,000. Perley Bell has been working on his design for many years and, according to him, it "really works." His furnace is rather expensive. He also makes smaller space heaters.

The Thorne Windsor.

44096—

A hard coal, self-feeding, base heating stove with all modern devices; 2 sizes. The leg base, foot rails, top rim, swing top, name plate, upper front mica frame, knobs, hinge pins are nickeled. The flues extend around the entire bottom; the hot air flues are in the back corners and unite at the top for double heating, beautifully ornamented and a perfect stove of the first class, and we guarantee it in every respect. Height given

44096
includes top ornament; height of ornament, 12 in.

Size.	Height.	Shipping weight.	Firebox.	Price, each.
11	54	290 lbs.	11x10x7	$19.40
13	60	340 "	13x11x7	22.88

CHAPTER SIX

WOODBURNING AND THE ENERGY CRISIS

"One of the major contributions to the global environmental crisis is our misuse of energy and our inability to harness certain energy sources. Our country is one of the primary culprits in the crisis, but there are many people who would like to participate in the solution. One means of participating is to develop an active relationship with the natural environment."
Bruce Anderson

"We could have all the energy we need, economically, and very soon, if we wanted to get it on with solar energy."
William Heronemus

"That's the whole point about thermodynamics, you have to fit all the parts together in an optimized way. Here it will make sense to use a windmill, here a little waterwheel, in another place it will make sense to burn wood, in another to have a diesel engine with a solar booster. Marvelous things can be done."

Barry Commoner,
The Country Journal, June 1976

What is the energy crisis, anyway? Does anybody know? We've all heard lots of different opinions, and no doubt we've formed some ourselves, but very few people have been able to understand the situation in any depth.

Most of us probably feel that the issue is too technical and complicated for us. This is unfortunate because the handwriting is on the wall, and what is more, it is in plain and understandable English!

Numerous government reports have been published, designed to "brief" our congressmen and other interested parties and provide them with all the pertinent information gathered by various governmental and private research organizations.

Congressmen are busy people. Many of them lack even college level training in the physical sciences. For this reason, perhaps for other reasons as well, these reports have been made very simple and self-explanatory. Anyone wishing to become at least as well-educated as a congressman with respect to the energy crisis can write to the United States Energy Research and Development Administration, Washington, D.C. 20545, and request all relevant information, especially "A National Plan For Energy Research, Development and Demonstration: Creating Energy Choices For the Future (Parts 1 & 2)." The United States Congress Office of Technology Assessment has published "An Analysis of the ERDA Plan and Program" which gives a much more balanced perspective on the situation. In this report, almost all the assumptions of the Energy Research and Development Administration are called to task, many questions are asked, and many alternatives are proposed. In addition, several critiques of the ERDA plan from sources outside the government are presented. This report is free for the asking. Just write to the United States Congress Office of Technology Assessment, Washington, D.C. 20510.

In our opinion, the energy situation is so crucial to how we shall be living during the coming decades that these documents should be mailed to every registered voter. But no intelligent attempt has been made to let people know that they even exist. It is unfortunate, but the chief source of information most of us are apt to receive concerning the energy situation comes, directly or indirectly, from the propaganda efforts being made by various interested powers. This information is designed to obscure the facts and distract the public with such obvious oversimplifications that once you start to understand the situation you will find in these propaganda masterpieces, often cleverly disguised as ads for oil companies and public utilities, a source of amusement to rival the funny papers.

What is not so funny is that such information often accomplishes with amazing efficiency exactly what its authors intend it to. Therefore we would like to mount a propaganda effort of our own. Although we are no match for the Madison Avenue advertising agencies, we think we have an edge, based only on our assumption that anyone who has read this far in our book will possess enough intelligence and imagination to realize how essential this information can be in helping to form realistic decisions concerning energy choices for the future.

At the risk of being somewhat less than completely objective we shall attempt to make our points clear and dramatic.

It is our contention that there is no energy shortage, but it is evident that we are going to have to pay quite a price. The decisions we make, and allow to be made for us, will determine just what kind of price we do have to pay.

If it is true, as we say, that there is no energy shortage, then why has the federal government created a multi-billion dollar agency, the Energy Research and Development Administration, to study the problem?

Good question! We don't know the answer to this one just yet. We have our suspicions and we are very curious. Supposedly ERDA has been mandated by various Acts of Congress to develop a comprehensive plan for energy research, development, and demonstration. In its summary report ERDA has claimed that there is an alarming prospect in the very near future of severe depletion of just those energy resources upon which we are currently most dependent: oil and natural gas. According to ERDA, production of domestic oil will begin to drop rapidly in the mid-1980's, as will the production of natural gas.

According to ERDA then, there is an energy shortage.

This is questionable. Estimates of the United States Geological Survey indicate that ERDA could be underestimating the amount of petroleum reserves yet available. Biologist Barry Commoner, in a series of articles published by "The New Yorker Magazine" (February 2, 9, and 16, 1976), suggests that if the problem is studied with a more comprehensive interpretation of the laws of physics, much greater efficiencies can be achieved in our use of *all* sources of energy. Professor Commoner concludes his arguments by speculating that the villain in the energy drama is the profit motive. He claims that the rational ideal would be for the economic system to be dependent on the requirements of the production system, which would, in turn, conform to the requirements of the ecosystem. In classic "cart before the horse" tradition, we seem to have developed just the opposite: the ecosystem is being systematically laid waste by a production system that is geared to generate a large amount of profit on the money invested. Professor Commoner exposes many interesting considerations which could be quite valid. It is the overall thoroughness of his assessment of our national energy situation which is so refreshing. But even if this assessment should prove to be incorrect, misinformed, or misinterpreted, it encourages us to take a closer look at the plans and policies of ERDA.

There are five energy goals proposed by ERDA which may constitute the Nation's energy policy:

1. To maintain the security and independence of the Nation;

2. To maintain a strong and healthy economy, providing adequate employment opportunities and allowing the fulfillment of economic aspirations (especially in the less affluent parts of the population);

3. To provide for future needs so that life styles remain a matter of choice and are not limited by the unavailability of energy;

4. To contribute to world stability through cooperative international efforts in the energy sphere;

5. To protect and improve the Nation's environmental quality by assuring that the preservation of land, water, and air resources is given high priority.

According to the summary report, we must act to develop every possible energy resource to meet these goals. If we compare this rhetoric with the allocation of ERDA's funding, however, it is clear that an overwhelming priority is being given to only those alternatives which will tend to maximise profits and taxes, at the highest corporate levels. It would seem that ERDA's nearest and dearest interests lie in the creation of a vast central electric grid fueled by nuclear reactors.

But there is rapidly growing public opposition to nuclear power generation. Virtually no progress has been made in resolving any of the very critical safety questions, and it is becoming clear that the costs are escalating beyond the point where freedom of life styles would be worth the price.

Nevertheless, the federal government nuclear bailout program is going full tilt and, unless we develop a movement similar to the one that brought a halt to American intervention in Vietnam, we can expect our costs of energy to go up, up, up.

The interesting feature of the ERDA plan is that in an age of dramatically changing energy developments it remains the bastion of the status quo by insisting that "life styles remain a matter of choice." This is a very devious statement. If we think about its implications, it becomes obvious that people such as the heads of oil companies and high-ranking government officials have a greater choice of life style than "the less affluent parts of the population."

The brazen hypocrisy of the ERDA plan is classic in its polarized simplicity. How it can be claimed that the Nation's environmental quality will be protected and improved by a major reliance on nuclear generation, with the question of long-term storage of radioactive wastes completely unresolved, tempts the limits of the imagination. Even more astounding is ERDA's consistent rejection of proposed solar energy projects which have even the slightest indication of being of direct benefit to the people.

The deeper one looks into the role ERDA is playing the clearer the picture becomes. National and international energy priorities are rapidly and dramatically changing. Who is threatened by this change? Everyone who depends upon the use of energy sources which are affected by the changing market conditions. But there is a great difference between the way in which people are threatened. Those of us who are energy consumers are threatened with our survival. How long can we stay healthy without a means of keeping warm? The people who are energy suppliers, however, are threatened with the loss of their positions of power. The interesting difference is that these people are much quicker to realize what is at stake and to attempt to shift their power so that they remain in control. The big pawn in the game is nuclear energy, the ultimate symbol of total personal power.

ERDA was created to replace the old Atomic Energy Commission, which was beginning to draw a considerable amount of flak. There has been very little change, however, in the people involved. Most of the staff of ERDA has been drawn from the old AEC. The significant difference is that these people now have the power, not only to push for nuclear development, but to squelch alternative technology as they see fit.

What lends a greater seriousness to the extent of this horrendous power monopoly is the degree to which the government agencies are working hand in glove with private interests. William E. Heronemus, one of the few people who thoroughly understand the full potential of alternate energy technology, and who also has a well-informed grasp of where the real resistance to implementing this technology lies, has offered the following comment on the 1975 solar energy policy:

> *"We will not tolerate any significant demonstration of alternatives to nuclear power using federal funds prior to 1985 because the existing congress — industry — national laboratories — university — complex, growing fat on nuclear, has no intention of loosing control over energy related funds."*

Extending the line of reasoning a bit further, it is possible to see that in many ways almost every person in the country is bound by anything from small habits to major life commitments to lend support to established social patterns which support the aims of the power brokers. Mr. Heronemus is of the opinion that we can effectively work as individuals to persuade our representatives in government to take a new look at our energy priorities. On the federal level, this is quite a task due to the fact that such a great number of congressmen are succeptible to the almost irresistable influence of the powerful established energy interests. Undoubtedly a good house-cleaning (and Senate cleaning) is in order.

Perhaps some people will want to argue this point. They will refer to numerous government backed solar and geothermal projects now underway. We challenge those people to show us one government-sponsored project which will demonstrate that solar heating and cooling can now be incorporated in residential construction at a net cost no greater than current oil burning systems, fuel included. Such projects, privately sponsored, are already completed and working. The Tyrrell House, shown in appendix IV, is an excellent example. Is this not the breakthrough that the public has been waiting for? Is this not the type of demonstration project the government should sponsor? Of course not! Why not? Because there's no money in it for the government, that's why. Thanks to a small engineering firm, a small local contractor, and the local bank, the Tyrrell family is home scot-free, and the utilities and the government can look elsewhere for their rate increases and corporate taxes.

They don't have to look far. Here's the rest of us, up to our ears in the sensational news of the day, heating with oil and already feeling the pinch. What will the situation be like in ten years? Is there anything we can do?

As a nation, we seem to be too eager to be reassured that "things will work out" to avoid the desperate manipulations of those for whom a choice of life style means living at fantastic advantage over the rest of us.

As individuals we have several very satisfactory alternatives available to us, and a distinct choice of life style, if we care to make the choice.

First and foremost is the use of solar energy for heating and cooling. The necessary technology has now been developed so that solar heating can be adapted to our style of building at a cost comparable to current rates for electric heat. For those intrepid enough to adapt their style of building to the requirements of solar technology, these costs can be reduced to less than current rates for oil burning.

Please do not be misled by these generalizations. There are many pitfalls awaiting the unwary. Headstrong engineers and unscrupulous contractors can quickly allow costs to run out of sight, with no assurance that the final product will work as predicted. Do-it-yourselfers can trim down expenses considerably but the risks of unsatisfactory performance are increased.

What we are saying is that successful houses have been built. You can find out where they are and go and visit them in the middle of winter and get the feel of them in operation. By this "visceral approach," prospective homeowners can be assured of harnessing the sun's energy to provide maximum independence from future "energy crises."

It is unfortunate, but the benefits of solar energy are more available to new buildings that can be engineered to make maximum use of the new technology. What can be done for those of us who are stuck with our old-fashioned gas, oil, or electrically heated homes? With mortgages and rising operating costs eating up our salaries, can we afford to do anything except go along with the "wait and see what happens" attitude toward the energy crisis?

Well, how far are we from the nearest woodlot?

Once we see what kind of game ERDA is playing we have only to observe that they do not even mention wood as a source of energy to wonder if there might be some real potential here.

The fact is that wood is historically our most familiar and reliable fuel. Furthermore, it poses no great environmental problems. Dr. Vincent J. Schaefer, the foremost authority on air pollution, says that "Man has accustomed himself to wood smoke." However, Dr. Schaefer agrees that if we can eliminate smoke through total combustion, so much the better.

The fact that many homeowners will spend as much money on a fireplace as they will on a heating system shows that something in us positively loves a fire. Finally, the remarkable breakthrough in high-efficiency wood burning now reaching maturity makes wood a cheaper source of heat than electricity or oil at current prices.

Let's go into the information supporting these assertions in greater detail, not so much to adduce our proofs, as to indicate ways in which we should be regarding energy resources in the years to come.

The graph in figure 44 is taken from the ERDA plan: "Creating Energy Choices For The Future." It shows that fuel wood supplied over 90% of our national energy needs in the year 1850. By 1885, coal was taking over and reached its peak in the early 1900's, about twenty five years after oil was first produced. By 1945 coal was being replaced by oil and natural gas, which have continued strong until recently.

Notice that wood has disappeared from the picture in recent years, while nuclear is the rising star.

The ERDA graph can be easily misinterpreted, however. For one thing, it refers to the *percentage* of energy consumption rather than the actual amounts. In the second place there is no indication that wood is the only indicated resource which is renewable. It is, and has been, our major living energy resource from time immemorial.

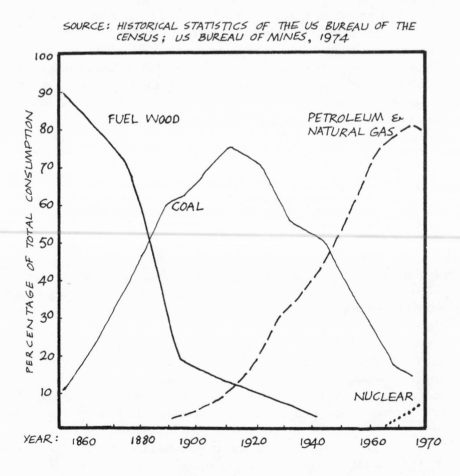

Figure 44   ENERGY CONSUMPTION PATTERNS

Figure 45 is a graph based on the total *amount* of energy consumption. It shows that, far from having sunk into oblivion, wood is being used as much now as it was in 1850. Somehow this doesn't stand to reason. In all likelihood it would be very difficult to come up with a graph which accurately displayed the true situation. It is useful to notice, however, that all of these graphs indicate that the oil and gas upon which we presently rely are by no means sacred, being relative newcomers on the scene. Imagine what position they would occupy if we were to chart a graph including all times since early civilizations.

Figures 45 and 46 indicate the potential that is currently going unused in our forest resources. In figure 46 notice that whereas we currently produce about 2 quads (quadrillions of BTU's) worth of energy in the pulp and paper industry, about the same amount of fossil-fuel energy is expended to accomplish this. In essence we are wasting all 16 quads of our yearly biomass growth.

Figure 46 shows that with intelligent management of, and increased emphasis on, intensive forestry use we could possibly increase our annual production of biomass growth by five times its current (and unused) capacity. We could double our wood and paper production and supply ten times as much productivity to the food and chemical industry and still have 58 quads of energy for use as a fuel. Bear in mind that this is a

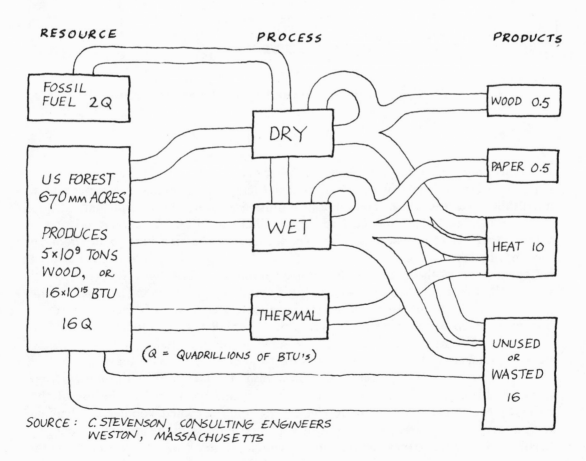

Figure 45   WOOD USE IN THE USA FOR 1975

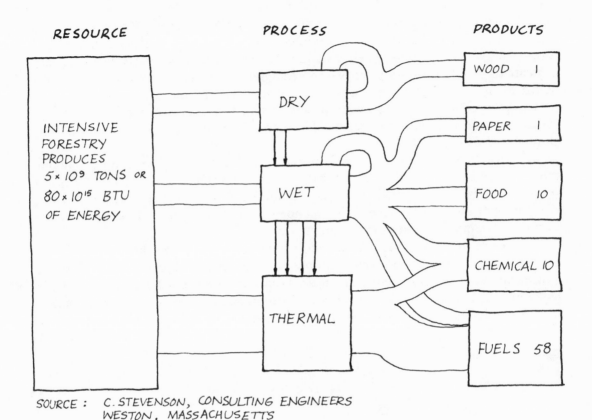

RESOURCE   PROCESS   PRODUCTS

SOURCE : C. STEVENSON, CONSULTING ENGINEERS
WESTON, MASSACHUSETTS

Figure 46   PROJECTED WOOD USE IN THE USA FOR 2000

possibility, not necessarily a probability; but when we consider that 58 quads represents over three quarters of our total annual energy requirements it becomes a very interesting possibility which should not be dismissed without very careful study.

Many people have looked into the possibility of increasing our use of wood as a fuel. Larry Gay, in "Heating With Wood," devotes the first part of the book to showing that there is enough fuelwood, if it could be spread around, to heat at least half, perhaps all, of the houses in the country without depleting the forests.

The catch here is in the phrase, "if it could be spread around". Much of the great "biomass growth" we've been crowing about, occurs well off the beaten track, inaccessible even to four-wheel drive vehicles. To think that such fuel wood could be easily cut, split, dried and delivered to the suburbs would be naive. But it is equally naive to assume that the problems of harvesting and delivery are prohibitive.

United States Congressman Hamilton Fish, Jr. has received a proposal (from us) that capable welfare and unemployment recipients be trained in the use of the necessary equipment and set to improving the government owned woodlands by culling out the less productive trees, many of which are interfering with the growth of younger, healthier trees, and cutting them up for firewood. Money from the sale of the cordwood could eventually more than offset the costs of welfare payments.

Unfortunately, Congressman Fish has not been able to develop such a proposal. Presumably he is concentrating his efforts on getting his National Nuclear Reappraisal Act, which calls for a five-year moratorium on construction of nuclear power plants until such time as they can be proven safe beyond question, out of committee and passed into law.

If any of our readers has a Congressman, State Senator or Assemblyman, or other appropriate government official in need of a good cause, here's one for the asking.

Even if the great "army of the unemployed" cannot be counted upon in this time of urgent need to bring out the wood, we are still not without recourse. We still have our machines; machines can do it!

Can there be any doubt? Let us hasten to assure you that machines can not only greatly increase the efficiency of logging operations, they are already doing it. May we introduce you now to just a few of these exciting machines: the feller-buncher, the grapple skidder, and the whole tree chipper.

A feller-buncher is a machine that performs the two operations indicated by its name. It fells trees with hydraulically operated shears, snipping off the tree much like garden shears snip off a flower stem. Simultaneously, it grasps the tree trunk, then lifts the entire above-ground portion of the tree, and lays it on the ground where it will lay the next trees all in a bunch, ready for the grapple skidder. Accumulators are optional attachments for feller-bunchers. They accumulate several felled trees before they need to be laid down in a bunch. In small timber, production can be doubled or tripled by using this attachment. By observation of the writer, feller-bunchers are capable of felling the above-ground portions of trees with minimum amounts of damage to the residual stand. Their bunching capability enables skidder operation to be much more efficient.

Grapple skidders have a grapple claw on the back which enables the operator to remain seated while picking up or dropping a bunch of trees or logs. In contrast, cable skidders require the operator to dismount and attach or unhitch the individual trees or logs. Because of this, grapple skidders have improved efficiency over other skidding methods by at least one-third, while reducing operator fatigue. They hold the load together, minimizing soil erosion and damage to the residual stand.

The machines developed for the purpose of chipping the trees have become known as Total Tree Chiparvestor (trademark of a machine made by Morbark Industries) or whole tree chippers, even though they don't use the below-ground portion of a whole tree. Of all the various machines necessary for the different methods of above-ground tree harvesting, the one machine necessary for any method is the so-called whole tree chipper. It is a portable machine, which can be moved easily right out to the landing in the forest by a truck tractor. After above-ground portions of trees are skidded to it, they are picked up by a powered arm with a claw and fed to a powered roller which moves the tree toward a revolving set of blades. The matchbook size chips can be blown directly into a trailer van. A chipper can fill a 45′ trailer in 14 minutes, but an average time would be 20 to 30 minutes. The chipper can be set up or ready to be moved in less than 15 minutes.

These machines, currently in use by New England pulp and paper industries were part of a comprehensive study submitted by J.P.R. Associates, Stowe, Vermont, to the Vermont State Department of Forests and Parks, to determine the feasibility of generating electricity in the State of Vermont using wood as a fuel. According to the authors:

> *"Progress is often defined in terms of the development of increasingly complex technologies which are often heavily reliant on non-renewable resources. The other side of the progress coin is that we are disdainful of outmoded ways of the past.*
>
> *As we approach what may be the end of the era of fossil fuels, those two sides may experience a reversal. Developments in recent years invite a reanalysis of our situation, particularly in regard to our energy needs.*
>
> *The mainstay of Vermont's economy, indeed of the economy of western civilization, is cheap, available fossil fuels. As a source of energy, petroleum is used to move our cars and trucks, to heat our homes and to produce our most versatile energy form, electricity. Once considered inexhaustible, oil has shown that it, like other non-renewable resources, has an end that is the dark at the end of a currently well-lit tunnel. In addition to being in short supply, oil has become a lever in the game of international politics and economics in which, by virtue of our dependence, we become permanent participants.*
>
> *Alternatives generally unavailable to whole nations may be viable as partial solutions at a regional and state level. Certainly those alternatives include solar, wind, and water, but for Vermont the time may be right for a revival of its traditional reliance on wood as a fuel."*

Among other findings it was determined that: "The Vermont forest produces an annual surplus of wood sufficient to generate Vermont's total electrical needs, and the economy of whole above-ground tree harvesting yields whole tree chips at a reasonable price."

Encouraged by such research, the newly formed Wood Energy Institute, a group of interested individuals primarily from the New England area, is attempting to initiate a pilot project demonstrating the feasibility of wood-fueled electrical generation. Far from being considered impractical or far-fetched, the Wood Energy Institute's plan is being given thoughtful consideration by both public utilities and certain governmental agencies.

This is an encouraging affirmation of the capacity of our forest reserves, especially when the fact is considered that there is more available hardwood produced in the Central States than there is in New England, but it gives rise to another specter: if tree-chewing machines come crawling through the woods, relentlessly feeding giant electric plants, what will be left for the wood stove?

Answer, probably plenty; but before we lose any sleep over this one, let's see how the Wood Energy Institute fares in obtaining federal funding for a pilot project. It would have to do much better than solar heating advocates have done so far, even if wood was considered as an available new energy source. At present ERDA has no such recognition of wood as a fuel.

So far as we can see, the best hope the Wood Energy Institute might have is that its proposed use of our wood resources could be rather wasteful. Consequently, such a program can be very easily used to discredit the use of wood as a source of energy. Should the Federal agencies fail to put the taxpayer's money at the disposal of the Institute, assistance might be looked for directly from the nuclear power folks.

Of course anyone interested in investing in his own fuel business has only to buy a few acres of woods. A suitable stand of hardwoods is supposed to yield a cord a year per acre on a renewable basis. Much depends on what is meant by "suitable stand". A productive woodlot management plan for cordwood production might be to leave the stumps of harvested trees to sprout. After a few years all but the dominant sprouts should be pruned, leaving the leader to shoot up, as the sole benefactor of the mature root system. If a woodlot were developed with fast-growing hardwood species resistant to root rot, fuel production would most likely exceed a cord per acre per year. White ash, about the best fast growing hardwood for this purpose, will regrow to harvest size in twenty years, and will easily produce more than a cord per acre per year.

There is an especially interesting consideration in this entire matter of how much wood we have available for fuel. That is the consideration of at what efficiency we intend to burn it. Whereas the net efficiency of electrical generation is somewhere around 30%, no matter what fuel is used, the home woodburner can now obtain efficiencies closer to 70%. If the feasibility of wood as a source of electrical generation is being seriously considered at 30% efficiency, imagine how much more available energy there is at 70% efficiency.

In our opinion, the biggest single factor contributing to the "credibility gap" in understanding the value of wood as a fuel, is the lack of common knowledge concerning the efficiency at which it can be burned. By making use of the concepts of matching a fuel to its most thermodynamically appropriate use, as advocated by Barry Commoner in his book, *The Poverty of Power*, we can not only greatly increase the amount of usable energy available from our forest resources, but we can reduce the cost as well.

The two graphs shown in figures 47 and 48 compare the cost of available heat units (net usable Btu's) and plot the break even point between wood burned at various efficiencies and the cost of electricity or oil. To determine the break even point, just find the current cost of oil or electricity in the horizontal scale and then go directly up the chart to the line representing the efficiency of your wood heater. When you reach this line, look over to the vertical scale to see how much you can afford to pay for a cord of wood to break even. The graphs show that if oil costs fifty cents a gallon you can afford to pay $85 a cord for wood at 60% efficiency, and still be coming out ahead; when electricity costs 5¢ a killowat hour you can afford to pay $230 a cord for wood.

Careful study of these charts will enable you to understand why we said earlier that a more efficient stove will repay almost any additional initial cost in time.

The charts also put into perspective the question of what will happen to the cost of wood as demand increases. Obviously wood should cost more as time goes on. The fact that firewood prices in our area are, at this writing, no higher than they were two years ago, is somewhat of a mystery. We suspect that our local wood dealers, living close to the land with no corporate financing or taxes to contend with, have not felt as insecure in the face of the energy crisis as the big fuel companies and the public utilities.

What is most interesting is that with no assistance from big government and completely unpromoted by big business, thousands upon thousands of Americans are quietly establishing their personal energy independence by renewing their connection with wood, mankind's oldest and most reliable fuel.

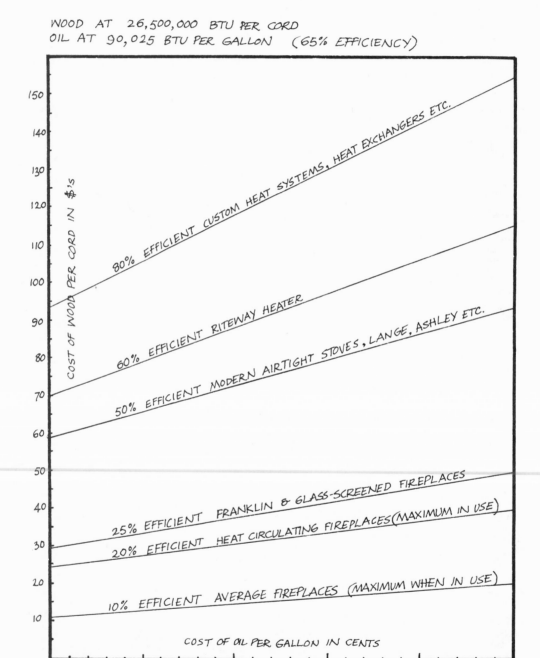

Figure 47 COMPARISON OF WOOD AND OIL COSTS

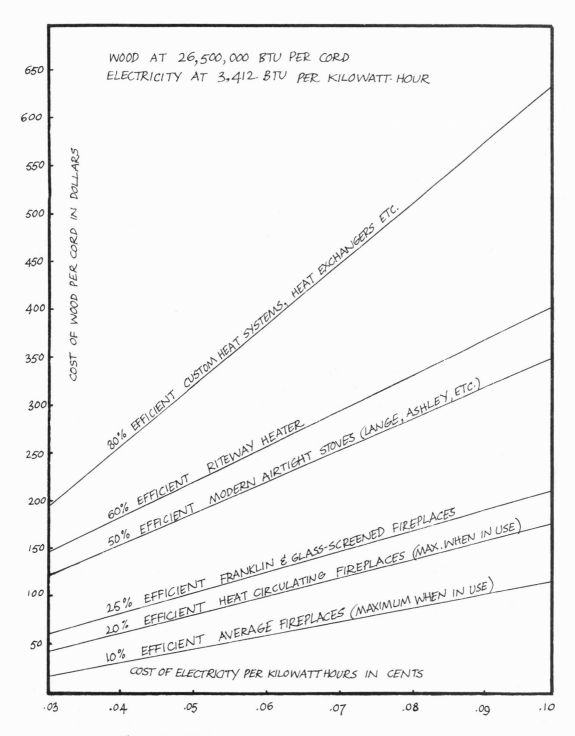

Figure 48   COMPARISON OF WOOD AND ELECTRICITY COSTS

Ward Windsor with Oven.

44095 The oven on this stove is guaranteed to work perfectly; it is placed close to the fire box, and the top oven plate is on a line with the top of the fire pot, so that there is an abundance of heat for baking and boiling with an ordinaary fire. We claim that we have secured a practical one without destroying the beauty of the stove. We do not furnish tea kettle as shown in cut. Height, with top ornament, 62 inches. Height, without top ornament, 50 inches.

Size.	Shipping weight.	Fire box.	Price
2	465 lbs.	13x10x8	$32.00

APPENDIX I

MAJOR MANUFACTURERS AND IMPORTERS

STOVES

Firm	Product
Ashley Automatic Heater Company 1604 17th Avenue, S.W., Box 730 Sheffield, Alabama 35660	Ashley space heaters
Atlanta Stove Works Atlanta, Georgia	All types of cast-iron stoves
Autocrat Corporation New Athens, Illinois 62264	Cooking ranges and space heaters
Bell, Perley Grafton, Vermont	Stoves and furnaces
Birmingham Stove and Range Company Box 3593 Birmingham, Alabama 35202	Many kinds of stoves, heaters, and ranges
Brown Stove Works, Inc. Cleveland, Tennessee 37311	Space heaters
C & D Distributors, Inc. Box 766 Old Saybrook, Connecticut 06475	Steel box stove
Cummings, Waldo G. Fall Road East Lebanon, Maine 04027	Furnaces
The Dam Site Stove Company R.D. no. 3 Montpelier, Vermont 05602	The Dynamite stove

Sam Daniels Company
Box 868
Montpelier, Vermont 05602

Wood burning furnaces

Duo-Matic
2413 Bond Street
Park Forest South, Illinois 60466

Multi-fuel furnaces

Fawcett Division, Enheat Ltd.
Sackville, New Brunswick, Canada

Cast-iron box, Franklin, parlor, and cookstoves

Fireview Distributors
Box 370
Rogue River, Oregon 97537

Improved barrel stoves

Fisher Stoves
504 S. Main
Concord, New Hampshire 03301

The Fisher stove

Garden Way Research
Department 64456
Charlotte, Vermont 05445

Steel box stove

Gay, Larry
Marlboro, Vermont

Steel box stove, accessories

H. D. I. Importers
Schoolhouse Farm
Etna, New Hampshire 03750

German coal stoves

Heatilator Fireplace
Division, Vega Industries, Inc.
Mt. Pleasant, Iowa 52641

Heatilator fireplaces

Kickapoo Stove Works, Ltd.
Main Street, Box 14W
La Farge, Wisconsin 54639

Wood burning furnaces

King Stove and Range Company
Box 730
Sheffield, Alabama 35660

All kinds of stoves

Kristia Associates
Box 1118
Portland, Maine 04104

Jøtul stoves, Combi-fires, fireplaces, ranges, and built-ins

Marathon Heater Company, Inc. Box 165, R.D. 2 Marathon, New York 13803	The Logwood Furnace
Mohawk Industries, Inc. 121 Howland Avenue Adams, Massachusetts 01220	The Temp-Wood stove
"Old Country" Appliances Box 330 Vacaville, California 95688	Tirolia European range
Preston Distributing Company Whidden Street Lowell, Massachusetts	Chappee and other stoves, ranges, and accessories
Preway Wisconsin Rapids, Wisconsin 54494	Fireplaces
Portland Franklin Stove Foundry Company Box 1156 Portland, Maine 04100	Cast-iron stoves and ranges
Ram Forge Brooks, Maine 04921	Heavy steel box stoves, furnaces, and boilers
Ridgway Steel Fabricators, Inc. Box 382 Ridgway, Pennsylvania 15853	Hydroplace fireplaces and Hydrohearth grates
Riteway Manufacturing Company Box 6 Harrisonburg, Virginia 22801	Riteway stoves, multi-fuel furnaces and boilers (wood-coal-gas-oil)
Self Sufficiency Products One Appletree Square Minneapolis, Minnesota 55420	Sierra, Alaskan and Gibraltar IV heavy steel stoves
Shenandoah Manufacturing Company, Inc. Box 839 Harrisonburg, Virginia 22801	Shenandoah space heaters
Scandinavian Stoves, Inc. Box 72 Alstead, New Hampshire 03602	Lange Danish stoves, Tiba Swiss ranges

Southport Stoves, Division Howell Corporation   Morsø stoves
Boston, Massachusetts

Sunshine Stove Works   Steel box stoves
Callicoon, New York 12723

Tekton Design Corporation   Kedelfabrik-Tarm imported wood-oil
Conway, Massachusetts 01341   boilers

The Merry Music Box   Styria Austrian heaters and ranges
10 McKown Street
Boothbay Harbor, Maine 04538

United States Stove Company   All kinds of stoves
Box 151
South Pittsburgh, Tennessee 37380

Vermont Castings, Inc.   The Defiant stove
Prince Street
Randolph, Vermont 05060

Vermont Counterflow Wood Furnace   Wood burning furnaces
Plainfield, Vermont 05667

Washington Stove Works   Cast-iron stoves, and a variety of
Box 687   cooking ranges, including marine
Everett, Washington 98201   ranges

Wilson Industries   Multi-fuel furnaces
2296 Wycliff
St. Paul, Minnesota 55114

ACCESSORIES

Firm	Product
The Blacksmith Shop Box 15 Mt. Holly, Vermont 05758	Hand-forged fireplace tools
Blazing Showers Box 327 Pt. Arena, California 95468	Hot water heat exchangers
Calcinator Corporation Bay City, Michigan 48706	Magic Heat heat exchangers

Futura Enterprises
5069 Highway 45 South
West Bend, Wisconsin 53095

Powered wood splitters

Household Wood Splitter
P.O. Box 143
Jeffersonville, Vermont 05464

Powered hyrdraulic splitters

Patented Manufacturing Company
Bedford Road
Lincoln, Maine 01773

Slip On heat fins

Frank Raftery Distributors, Inc.
Box H
Belfast, Maine 04915

Katrina building panels and heat
shields

Riteway Manufacturing Company
Box 6
Harrisonburg, Virginia 22801

Floor mats and hot water devices for
stoves

Sturges Heat Recovery, Inc.
Stone Ridge, New York

Thriftchanger heat exchangers

Portland Willamette Company
6804 N.E. 59th Place
Portland, Oregon 97218

Glassfyre screens

Taos Equipment Manufacturers, Inc.
Box 1848
Taos, New Mexico 87571

Power splitter

Cook's Windsor for Wood.

Cook's Windsor, for wood only, has a door on each end of fire box, nickel ornaments, ground edges, large fire box, patent oven door opener, towel rod, heavy false bottom in fire box, a swing fender and outside nickel oven shelf.

44090 Plain Square, without reservoir, for wood only.

Size.	Oven.	Fire box.	Weight.	Price.
8-20	18x21x12	24x10 in.	275 lbs.	$14.00
9-20	20x21x12	24x10 "	275 "	14.58
8-22	20x22x12	26x11 "	300 "	16.20
9-22	22x23x12	26x11 "	300 "	16.75

44091 Cook's Windsor Stove with gray enamel reservoir.

Size.	Oven.	Fire box.	Weight,	Price.
8-20	18x21x12	24x10 in.	355 lbs	$19.45
9-20	20x21x12	24x10 "	355 "	21.00
8-22	20x23x12	26x11 "	380 "	22.80
9-22	22x22x12	26x11 "	380 "	23.37

The above prices do not include pipe shelf, as shown in cut.

44091½ Pipe Shelf to fit above stove (weight 35 lbs.). Price, extra..................................$3.25

APPENDIX II

INSTALLATION OF METAL PREFABRICATED CHIMNEYS

USING A CEILING SUPPORT PACKAGE

Tools you will need: plumb bob, brace and bit, or electric hand drill with 1/2" bit and extension, sabre saw or "sawzall" (can be rented) with 4" blade for cutting nail-embedded wood, carpenter's pencil or crayon, hand saw, square, stepladder or stool, tape measure, hammer, ladder to reach roof (if needed), utility knife, "wonder bar", screwdriver, and pliers.

Materials you will need in addition to the chimney components: one 8' long 2"x4", two dozen 8d nails, six 12d nails, one dozen 2 1/2" roofing nails, small tube of silicone seal, or can of plastic roofing cement.

1.   You are going to have to cut holes in the ceiling, and in any floors or ceilings above, 4" wider in diameter than the outside diameter of the metal pipe. If you are using a 6" chimney, for example, the outer diameter will be 8", so you would be cutting 12" holes. To keep the run as straight as possible, and to avoid misplaced holes, it is best to plan ahead, trying to measure floor joists, ceiling rafters, and roof rafters to be sure the holes will line up vertically. Often, the roof rafters are offset 1 1/2" from the ceiling rafters. If you have any doubts, drill a 1/2" hole in the approximate center of the larger hole and compare with a plumb bob. If you cannot tell what is above a ceiling in the way of rafters, etc. poke a finger through the test hole and feel around for a rafter. If you don't feel anything, enlarge the hole to admit your hand. If you do feel a rafter, still enlarge the hole, but keep away from the rafter.

2.   Once the holes are lined up, outline the final circumference of the big hole with a crayon and cut it out with a sabre saw. Do not cut through the roof yet.

3.   Frame in supports for the ceiling support package, (see figure 1). This is easy if you have access to the rafters from above. If they are closed in by flooring, you must fish the support headers up through the hole, mark their position, and toenail them in with 8d nails, being careful that they do not move too much off the mark. This will be easier if you cut them just a fraction longer than the distance you measure. Nailing in this position is quite awkward, but with patience it can be done. You may want to enlarge the hole in the ceiling a few inches in order to have more working room. Just be sure that the trim plate will cover what you cut out.

4.   Nail the ceiling support package to the supports with 8d nails. Read the instructions.

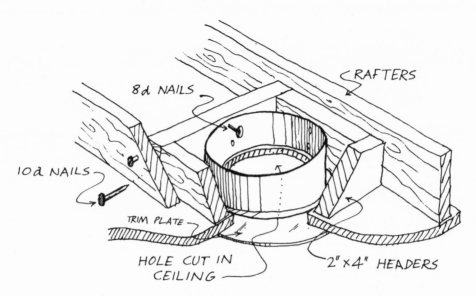

Figure 1   FRAMING OUT FOR CEILING SUPPORT

5.   Set the first section of chimney pipe down into the support package. Follow the directions of the manufacturer. If the pipe is to be exposed upstairs, you may want to slide a sheet-metal spacer over the first section to cover the hole in the floor, followed by a trim plate which can be slid up the pipe later, to cover the hole in the ceiling.

6.   Add sections of pipe one at a time, locking each one securely as you go. It is nice to have someone helping you with this. When you get within one section of the roof, drill a pilot hole up through the roof, and you are ready for the outdoor work.

7.   If you don't have a helper, try and anticipate what you will need in the way of tools and materials so you don't have to keep scrambling up and down the ladder.

8.   Once you are up on the roof and have located the pilot hole, cut away the proper amount of shingles using a utility knife.

9.   Cut out the hole in the sheathing with a sabre saw, making it a few inches wider at the top and bottom in the form of an ellipse. This should maintain 2″ clearance to the chimney.

10. Use the "wonder bar" to loosen sufficient nails in the shingles above the hole so that you can slide the flashing up under the shingles until it is lined up with where the chimney will be coming through.

11. Leaving the flashing loosely in place, slide the next section of pipe down and get it locked on below.

110

12. Add on the remaining sections of chimney, and install the cap and storm collar, as per the instructions.

13. Nail down the flashing with 2 1/2'' roofing nails, and apply a bead of roofing cement or, better yet, silicone-seal around the top of the storm collar and along the sides of the flashing.

14. Go back and fasten the trim plates. Before you do this you might want to pack the space around the pipe with fiberglass insulation to prevent drafts.

USING A ROOF SUPPORT PACKAGE

Tools you will need: all tools mentioned for ceiling support except plumb bob and square, plus a carpenter's level.
Materials you will need in addition to the chimney components: one dozen 2 1/2'' roofing nails, small tube of silicone seal or can of plastic roofing cement.

1. Decide where the chimney will go through the roof. This should be as close to midway between rafters as is possible. If you cannot tell where the rafters are from looking at the ceiling, go outside and see if you can find where the soffit fascia is nailed on. There's your rafter. If all else fails, use the finger probe technique explained earlier.

2. Drill a 1/2'' pilot hole up through the roof.

3. Making sure you have all the tools and equipment you need, go up on the roof and locate the pilot hole. Cut away all shingles and any insulation to allow for the hole. With Metalbestos brand also cut away to solid decking where support flanges will mount (see figure 2).

4. Use the "wonder bar" to loosen sufficient nails in the shingles above the hole to slide the flashing up under the shingles, until it is lined with where the chimney will be coming through.

5. Follow the manufacturer's instructions to mount the roof support unit. Check for plumb with a level before final securing. Metalvent brand roof support packages have straps which must be nailed from below. This is really only practical in new construction, where headers can be installed. For fitting to an existing house, the Metalbestos is much easier to work with.

6. After the roof support package is fastened, slide the flashing over the roof support package and up under the top shingles. If you have a mineral paper or tar roof, just put the flashing directly on top of the roof. After it is nailed down seal all the edges with hot tar or plastic roofing cement.

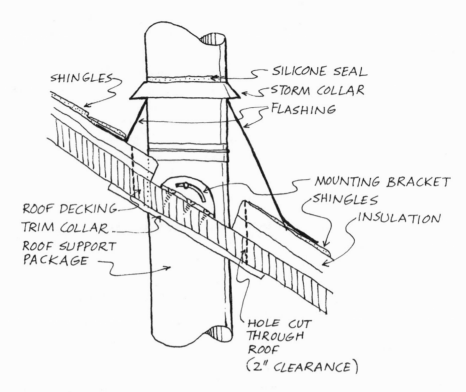

Figure 2   INSTALLATION OF CHIMNEY THROUGH ROOF

7.   Add on the remaining sections of chimney and install the cap and storm collar as per the instructions.

8.   Nail down the flashing with 2 1/2" roofing nails and apply a bead of roofing cement or silicone seal around the top of the storm collar and along the sides of the flashing.

9.   Back inside, fasten the trim plate to the ceiling and install the lower sections of the pipe.   Locking bands should be used to keep them from breaking loose in the future.

APPENDIX III

THE KERN BARREL STOVE

The following account takes apart each component of the stove and describes its separate fabrication. Although a particular size or gauge of metal for various parts may be specified, the builder should realize that his range of choices may vary widely, depending on what is conveniently at hand.

For instance, the gas combustion flue is specified to be 10 gauge, 7″ round steel well-casing. Theoretically, this flue should be heavier gauge, larger diameter cast iron, able to withstand the intense combustion heat encountered in this section of the stove. But while steel is easier to cut and weld than cast iron, well-casing is cheap and available. Furthermore, on Ken's prototype stove, the well-casing combustion flue proved to be entirely satisfactory.

The stove was designed so that any semi-skilled, metal working homesteader could fabricate the entire unit in his home workshop. This happened only partly by choice, for Ken's metal-working ability was limited by lack of experience and sophisticated tooling. A basic understanding of arc and gas welding techniques is, of course, essential. But even here, an expertly applied bead of weld is not essential when liberal quantities of furnace cement are available. Furnace cement made the whole project possible! It took a $2 pint-size can of this amazing material to cover the multitude of welding sins on the prototype stove alone.

STAND

Construction of the metal base support is self-explanatory in figure 1. The stand is anchored to the 55 gallon oil drum by four 3/8″ bolts, which fasten the angle iron frame directly to the two ribs found on most oil drums. Drill and tap the ribs to receive the 3/8″ bolts — two on each side.

COMBUSTION DRUM

A 4″ segment is first cut longitudinally out of a 35 gallon oil drum. This cut represents a chord length of 15″. When the plate-steel cooktop is welded to the cut surface there should be a net distance of 14″ from the bottom of the barrel to the cooktop.

The cooktop can now be welded to the combustion. Cut out the face of the

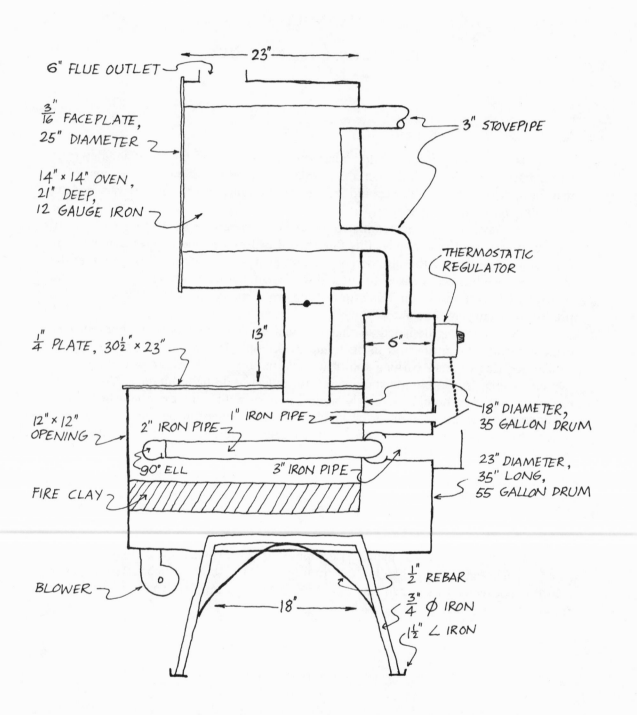

6" FLUE OUTLET

23"

$\frac{3}{16}$" FACEPLATE, 25" DIAMETER

3" STOVEPIPE

14" × 14" OVEN, 21" DEEP, 12 GAUGE IRON

THERMOSTATIC REGULATOR

$\frac{1}{4}$" PLATE, 30$\frac{1}{2}$" × 23"

13"

6"

12" × 12" OPENING

1" IRON PIPE

18" DIAMETER, 35 GALLON DRUM

2" IRON PIPE

90° ELL

3" IRON PIPE

23" DIAMETER, 35" LONG, 55 GALLON DRUM

FIRE CLAY

BLOWER

$\frac{1}{2}$" REBAR

$\frac{3}{4}$" ϕ IRON

18"

1$\frac{1}{2}$" ∠ IRON

Figure 1   KERN BARREL STOVE, SIDE VIEW

114

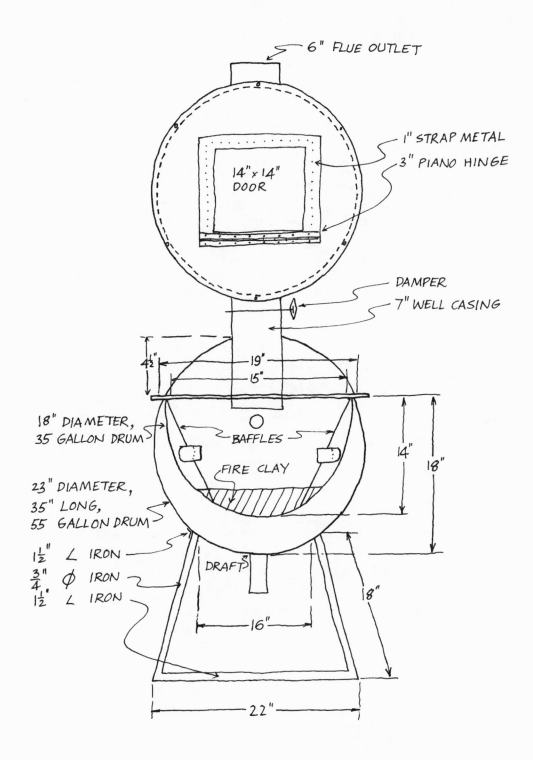

6" FLUE OUTLET

1" STRAP METAL

3" PIANO HINGE

14"x 14"
DOOR

DAMPER

7" WELL CASING

19"

15"

4½"

18" DIAMETER,
35 GALLON DRUM

BAFFLES

FIRE CLAY

14"

18"

23" DIAMETER,
35" LONG,
55 GALLON DRUM

1½" ∠ IRON

¾" ⌀ IRON

1½" ∠ IRON

DRAFT

16"

18"

22"

Figure 2   KERN BARREL STOVE, FRONT VIEW

combustion drum and drill or cut holes in back to receive the primary and secondary air intake pipes. Now you can weld the gas combustion flue in place. A connector flange is provided for attaching the oven assembly. Construction of this flange and details of the air pipes are shown in figures 3 and 4.

Figure 3   CONNECTOR FLANGE

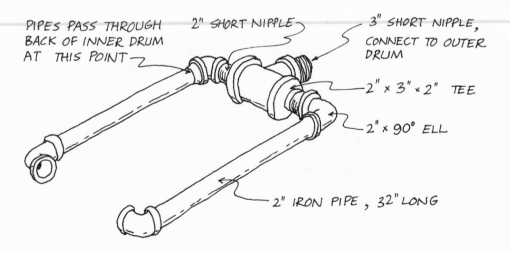

Figure 4   PRIMARY AIR PIPES

WARM AIR CHAMBER

The warm air chamber consists of a 55 gallon oil drum. A 5″ segment is cut out of the drum, establishing a chord length of 19″ and an 18″ distance between the bottom of the drum and the cooktop. Cut out the holes for the primary and secondary pipes, assemble the pipe sections that are to go between the combustion drum and the warm air chamber, and jockey the entire assembly together until the warm air chamber is in place and can be welded to the cooktop. The stand can now be bolted to the drum and the blower installed. Cut an opening for the fuel access door and connect the rest of the air supply pipe system. The pipes may be fastened mechanically with lock nuts and unions, or they may be welded in place. Once the primary air supply pipes have been installed at the sides of the combustion drum, position the baffle plates and pour the refractory cement base. When this has hardened, the fuel access door may be mounted. On the prototype model the fuel access door was salvaged from an old wood heater. One can also be made from 3/16″ steel plate, using a 3″ piano hinge. Silver Seal can be used to obtain an airtight seal.

OVEN

Smoke circulates between the outer shell and the actual oven chamber. To form the outer shell, cut a 1/3 section off a 55 gallon drum. Remove the lip from the discarded section and weld it to the drum edge. This provides a finished edge onto which the oven face plate can be bolted. The 3/16″ steel face plate is anchored to the outer oven shell with six 3/8″ bolts. Figure 5 shows how this is done. The oven chamber is welded directly to the face plate. When the outer chamber is used for smoking meats, the inner chamber must be removed.

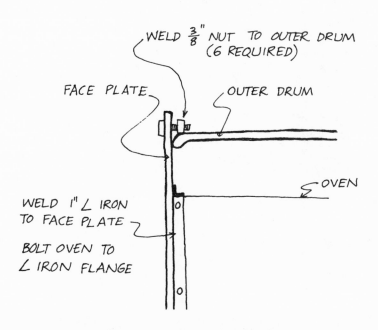

Figure 5   FACE PLATE DETAIL

OUTLETS

All that remains to complete the stove is the provision for smoke flue, dampers, and warm air outlets. A metal ring must be welded on the top of the outer oven shell to receive a 6″ stovepipe. For this you can recurve a 2″ section of well-casing. All warm air outlet pipes can be made from 3″ galvanized iron flue-pipe. A system of dampers is necessary if heat is to be supplied to other room areas. Finally, a damper must be constructed to regulate the primary draft. We had access to both a thermostatic regulator and magnetic damper from an old Riteway stove, which made things quite simple.

APPENDIX IV

HOUSES DESIGNED TO BE
HEATED BY WOOD

THE WEAVER HOUSE
WOODSTOCK, NEW YORK

The design of the Weaver House is a result of quite a bit of collaboration. The owner, Helen Weaver, is an artist. She started the planning herself, based on her own ideas of what she wanted, stimulated and fortified by much of what she had read in "The Owner Built Home" by Ken Kern.

By the time Helen came to me for consultation on the heating system and energy dynamics, the basic floorplan was already formulated. The significant change I made was to rotate the house 90° on its axis to allow greater use of supplemental solar heating through the windows and to present a virtually windowless wall to the north. Further protection against the cold north air is achieved by the addition of the woodshed which is quite handy to the stove.

The "air-lock" principle was employed by adding an entry-foyer, and by providing winter access to the deck through the greenhouse. In warmer weather the french doors are used. Due to the fact that the greatest amount of heat loss in most houses occurs through air exchange, the air-lock principle is more important for energy conservation than extra insulation.

All exterior walls are framed with 2"x6" members and insulated with 5 1/2" of fiberglass building insulation. This conserves heat, but the nicest feature is the resulting deep window sills provided by the thicker wall. Windows and sliding glass doors are of thermopane. The windows are equipped with interior insulated shutters or drapes wherever possible.

Credit for the amazingly compact (and therefore inexpensive) central plumbing wall must go to Ken Kern. The water storage tanks go under the darkroom bench. The central heating stove is a Riteway 2000. By means of a flat tank set on top of the Riteway, cold water can be preheated before going into the hot water tank.

The central masonry core carries the flue from the Riteway, a Count Rumford style fireplace, and a wood cookstove.

I charged Helen by the hour for my time and the total cost of designing the house came to $185. Later Helen and I built a scale model, for reasons not directly design-related, and discovered a few things not apparent on the plans. For one thing the masonry core tended to take up too much room, and it was subsequently moved across to the west wall, sacrificing the wood cookstove and some thermal mass. Personally, I didn't like the idea of moving the fireplace core, but Helen had a first class chimney built for the Riteway so I couldn't kick too much. After all, it is her house.

HOUSES DESIGNED TO BE HEATED BY WOOD/*The Weaver House*

The house was built on five beautiful wooded Woodstock acres in the summer of 1975. The woodshed, entry-foyer, greenhouse and insulated shutters have not been installed yet (1976). At the end of a full winter of colder than average temperatures, Helen estimated she used three and a half cords of wood for heating.

Figure 1   WEAVER HOUSE, SIDE ELEVATION

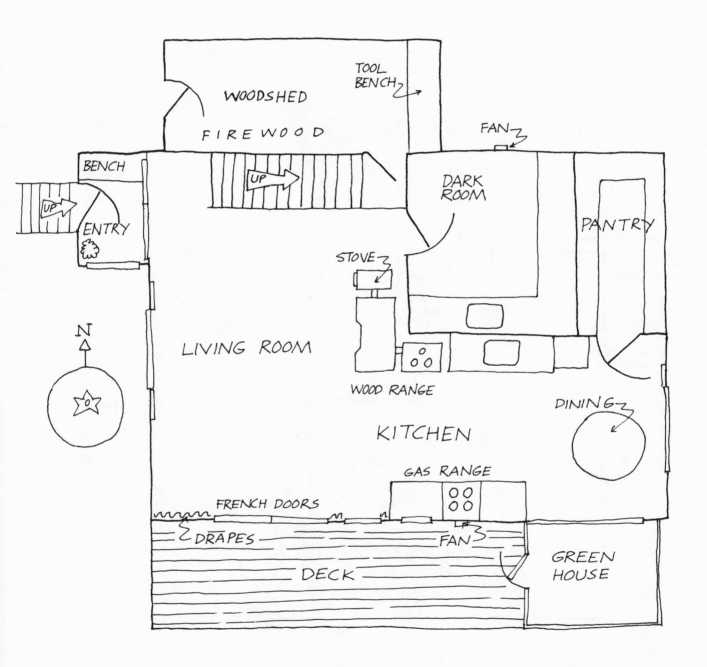

Figure 2   WEAVER HOUSE, FIRST FLOOR PLAN

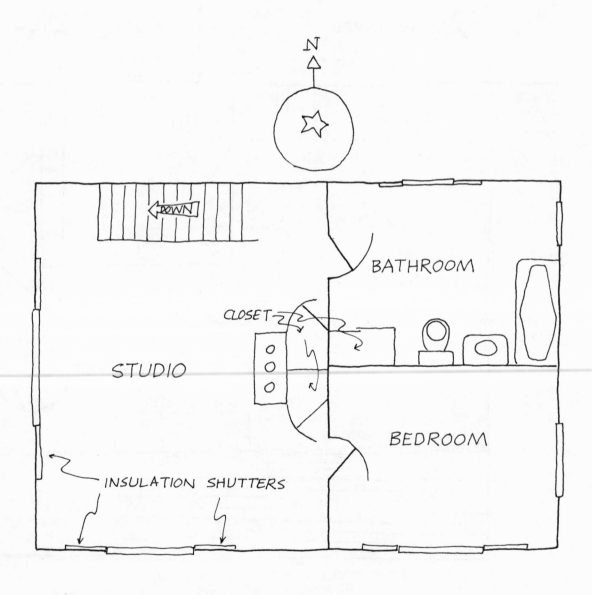

Figure 3   WEAVER HOUSE, SECOND FLOOR PLAN

THE WIDMAN HOUSE
PHOENICIA, NEW YORK

This house, unlike the other houses in this section, was not specifically designed to conserve energy. It was designed and built by Mike Earnest, an innovative builder of fine custom homes, to the exact requirements of the owner, who just happens to enjoy heating with wood stoves and fireplaces.

Since the house is used mostly on weekends, especially in the winter, considerations of maximum efficiency have played second fiddle to the esthetics. Nevertheless, the system is quite efficient.

The use of numerous woodburning appliances, and the centrally located masonry core, are reminiscent of the houses built by the early settlers, yet the house is a crisply contemporary design and the stoves are modern and efficient. By using multiple heaters, portions of the house which are used only periodically need not be heated all the time.

The Jøtul fireplace is an elaborately decorated cast-iron unit around which room air circulates, either passively or more vigorously, when a built-in fan is turned on. This distributes heat nicely around the living room, dining room and kitchen area, when a good fire is going. Were the fireplace to be equipped with glass screens, the same amount of heat could be obtained with a much smaller fire.

The first and third level living spaces are simply heated by the Jøtul stoves located there.

The intensity of the owner's enthusiasm for wood stoves is such that a glassed-in porch, which is being added to the east side of the house, will be equipped with a large Lange box stove in red enamel.

Figure 4   WIDMAN HOUSE, SOUTH ELEVATION

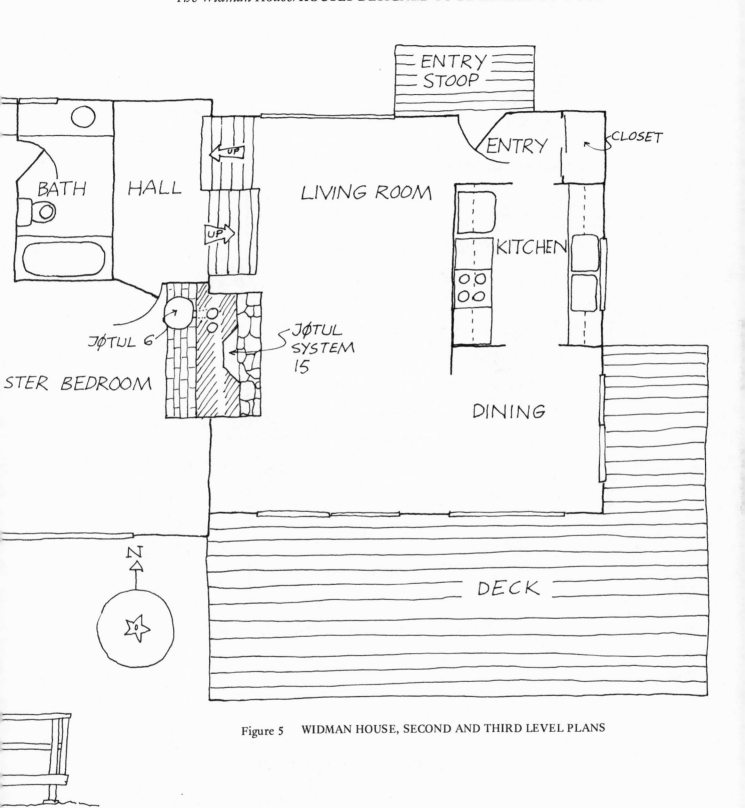

Figure 5   WIDMAN HOUSE, SECOND AND THIRD LEVEL PLANS

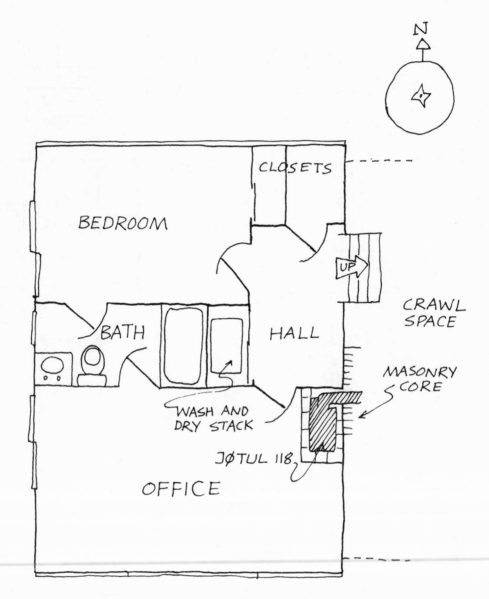

Figure 6   WIDMAN HOUSE, FIRST LEVEL PLAN

THE TYRRELL HOUSE
BEDFORD, NEW HAMPSHIRE

This three bedroom house combines solar heating and cooling with ecological principles and energy conservation. It circumvents most of the social and technological problems inherent in many solar heated buildings, and is also designed to have a minimal impact upon the site and be energy conserving. Solar collectors, instead of being tilted on a sloping roof, stand vertically in combination with south-facing windows, which have insulated shutters that close during sunless periods.

The building itself is designed as a solar collector. The south-facing windows admit solar heat during the day, and the heat is stored in the 4" concrete floor slab and the 8" and 12" concrete walls. The heat is then trapped in the house for use at night, and on cloudy days by the insulating shutters on the windows, and by massive amounts of insulation between the concrete and the earth, which is bermed up around the east, north, and west walls of the house.

The sun's heat is collected through the use of south-facing, vertical solar collectors in combination with windows. The sun penetrates through two layers of fiberglass-reinforced polyester sheet, strikes and heats a blackened 12" thick concrete wall similar to the Trombe-Michael solar system developed in France. The heat collected is then circulated into the house by natural air convection. As the warmed air rises in the space between the blackened concrete and the fiberglass sheet, it is ducted into the rooms at the ceiling height while simultaneously drawing cooler air in through a duct at the floor level. Warm air is ducted to the spaces on the north side of the house through operable panels located at the ceiling level in each room on the south side.

Heating and cooling diagrams are shown indicating the basic operation of the house during summer and winter. Auxiliary heating is provided by one wood cookstove and one wood heater within the home.

Cooling and ventilating are provided for by dampers which open on the north side of the building and by a dampering system inside the solar collector, which ducts the heated air through the collector to the outside while cool air is drawn in from the north side of the building.

Domestic hot water for the home is preheated by the solar collector before the water enters the electric hot water heater. The water supply line to the domestic hot water heater passes through about 75' of 3" PVC pipe embedded in the concrete collector wall. The pipe has about 30 gallons in water storage capacity.

Care has been taken during construction to minimize the effect upon the site, as well as to use recycled materials. Instead of letting water drain away from the site, it is captured and allowed to seep back into the soil on the site. On the south side, deciduous trees and movable, horizontal shading devices shade the building during summer, and allow the sunlight to penetrate and strike the solar collector in the heating season. Plumbing fixtures are chosen to use minimum amounts of water.

The house will use 10% to 20% of the energy customarily needed for heating and cooling homes in New Hampshire and for heating domestic hot water as well. The home requires 110,000,000 BTU's of heat energy per heating season. About 75% of this energy is provided by the sun. This is compared with 250,000,000 BTU's of heat energy required by a conventional home of the same size in the same climate.

The home is 25'x81', including a large double garage giving 2,025 square feet of gross floor area for the entire dwelling.

During the 1975 to 1976 heating season two and a half cords of medium hardwood (birch, maple, etc.) were used. Of this two and a half cords, one was used primarily for cooking, the other one and a half was used for supplemental heat. The average monthly electric cost for the hot water heater was $7.00.

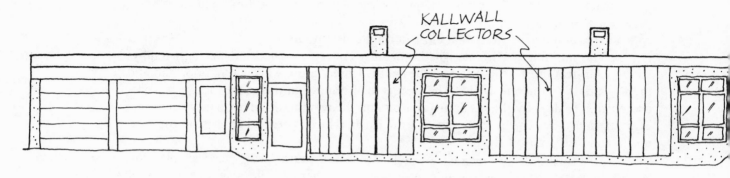

Figure 7   TYRRELL HOUSE, SOUTH ELEVATION

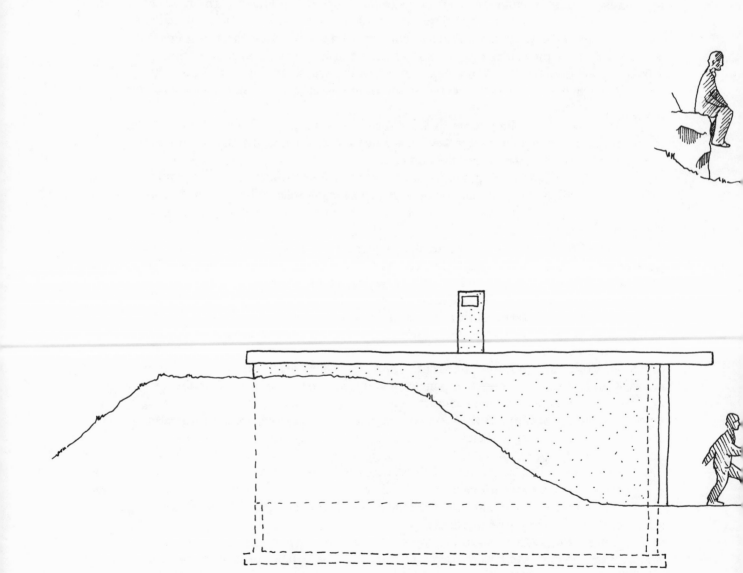

Figure 8   TYRRELL HOUSE, WEST ELEVATION

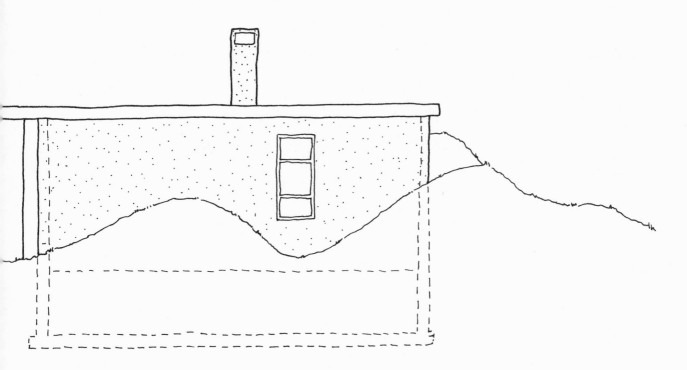

Figure 9   TYRRELL HOUSE, EAST ELEVATION

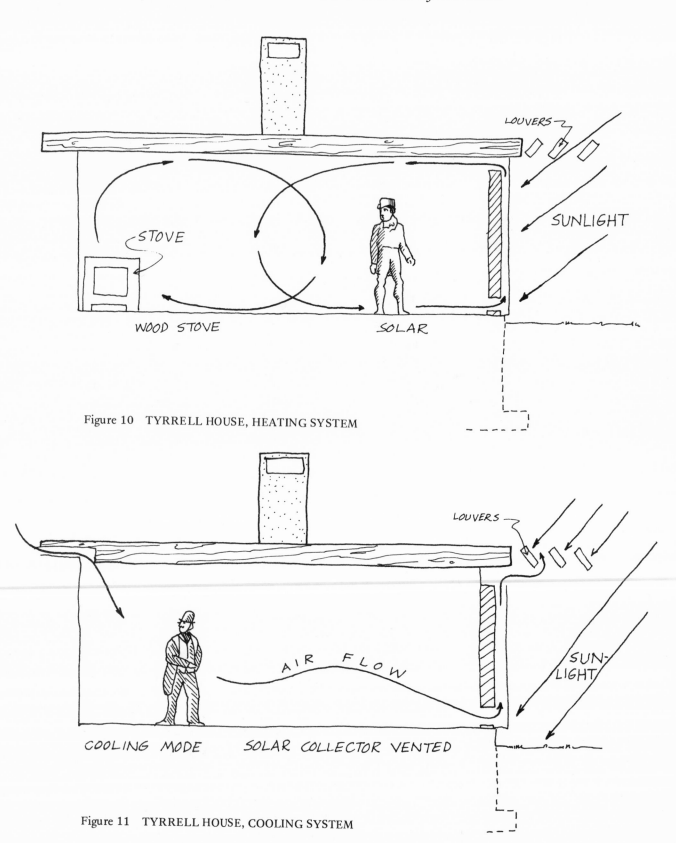

LOUVERS

SUNLIGHT

STOVE

WOOD STOVE

SOLAR

Figure 10   TYRRELL HOUSE, HEATING SYSTEM

LOUVERS

AIR FLOW

SUN-LIGHT

COOLING MODE   SOLAR COLLECTOR VENTED

Figure 11   TYRRELL HOUSE, COOLING SYSTEM

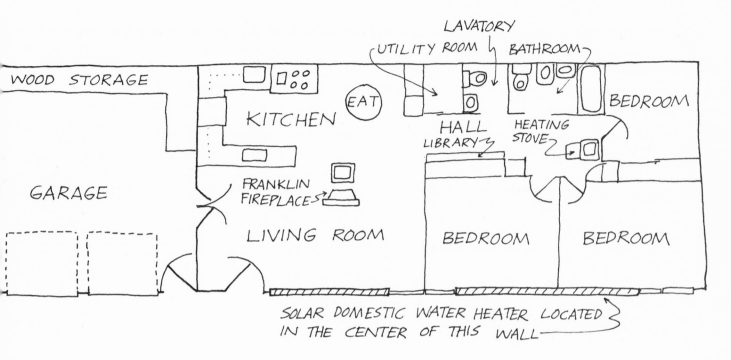

Figure 12   TYRRELL HOUSE, FLOOR PLAN

THE MAINE AUDUBON SOCIETY HOUSE
PORTLAND, MAINE

The new headquarters of the Maine Audubon Society, located at Gilsland Farm near Portland, Maine, is one of the first attempts to utilize alternate energy systems on a large scale.

The 5,500 square foot office building was designed by architect George Terrien, and features a heating system designed by Richard Hill of the University of Maine's Department of Industrial Cooperation. Solar and wood-fired heat are combined in an interlocking system designed to totally heat the building with renewable energy resources.

The heart of this system is a heat storage bed composed of 105 tons of crushed granite of an average diameter of 1″. The stones rest on a galvanized steel grate 70′ in length by 10′ in width. The stones are stacked to a height of 3′ along the grate. Heated air from the collectors and the wood furnace is circulated by fans along the vertical axis of the stone bed, rather than through the much longer horizontal axis, to reduce friction, and the energy used to circulate the heated air. The desirability of this storage bed was confirmed by preliminary tests.

A major development goal of this project has been the design of inexpensive but durable solar collectors that could be built by the homeowner or contractor. This goal has been achieved with a design that explodes some of the more common myths about solar collectors. The major emphasis of solar businesses and research groups has been to develop factory manufactured systems. Maine Audubon decided to see if a collector could be designed which a local building contractor or homeowner could put together right on the site — thus eliminating the factory middleman. This has two advantages: the fewer times a product changes hands, the less profit mark-up is put on the cost; secondly, thousands of building contractors (and therefore potential solar builders) already exist — compared to the handfull of solar companies making equipment. If contractors could make their own equipment, the whole process could be speeded up tremendously.

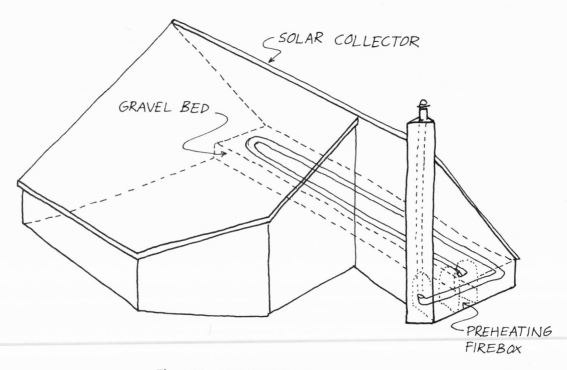

Figure 13   AUDUBON HOUSE, BASIC DESIGN

The Gilsland Farm building uses 2,000 square feet of these specially designed air-type collectors which will provide a projected 70% of the needed heat. Air, instead of water, was chosen as the medium to transfer the heat of the sun to the building, because blowing air through a collector system has fewer design problems than blowing water: no leaky joints, no miles of copper pipe carrying water across the heat transfer surface, no welding.

This is especially important because the units were designed for field construction. Air collectors also don't freeze up like water collectors and therefore no protection measures need be taken such as the use of anti-freeze, collector drainage systems, or secondary heat exchangers in storage areas.

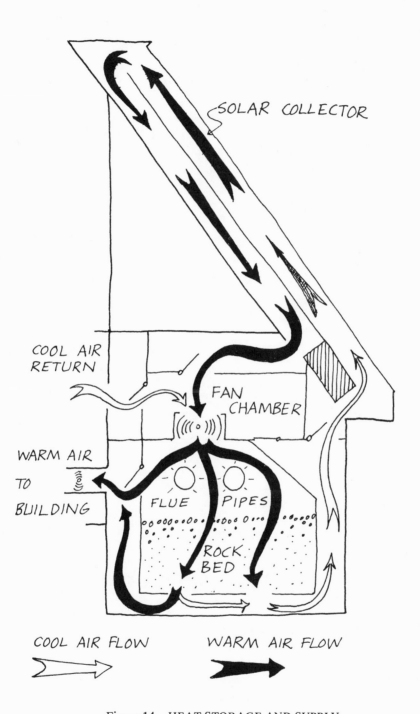

SOLAR COLLECTOR

COOL AIR
RETURN

FAN
CHAMBER

WARM AIR

TO

BUILDING

FLUE   PIPES

ROCK
BED

COOL AIR FLOW   WARM AIR FLOW

Figure 14   HEAT STORAGE AND SUPPLY

The cross section of a solar collector is shown in figure 15. One major difference from other air solar collectors is that instead of having a copper or aluminum absorption base, regular screen window type insect mesh was stapled onto black painted plywood. Air circulating through the collector passes through the insect screening and transfers the heat to the rock storage bed. The plywood base was chosen because contractors know the material well, and find it easier to use than sheet metals.

The collector cover is a fiberglass related product, manufactured by Kallwall Inc. of New Hampshire. This material is almost as good as glass in passing through sunlight to the insect screening, but far easier to work with and cheaper to buy. Because it is plastic, there are no breakage problems. When you need to fasten it to the collector you just drill through and screw the cover down.

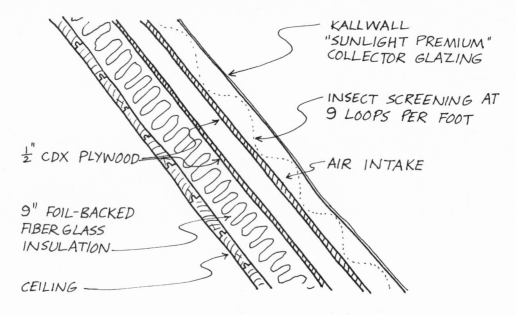

KALLWALL
"SUNLIGHT PREMIUM"
COLLECTOR GLAZING

INSECT SCREENING AT
9 LOOPS PER FOOT

AIR INTAKE

½" CDX PLYWOOD

9" FOIL-BACKED
FIBERGLASS
INSULATION

CEILING

Figure 15   CROSS SECTION OF SOLAR COLLECTORS

The cost for the collector figures out to $2.50 a square foot for materials, and an additional $1.50 a square foot for assembly by the contractor. Building these collectors is really no more difficult than putting a roof on, so labor costs, once a contractor has worked with systems a bit, might even be less than this figure.

As with the heat storage bed, the efficiency of the collector has been tested by designer Richard Hill and found to compare favorably with commercially made units available at twice the cost.

When additional heat is required the specially engineered wood furnace will be fired up. In designing the fabrication of this system, there were two basic goals:

1.   Separation of heat transfer from combustion.

Traditional wood furnace designs pass heat out the sides of the furnace directly into the rooms into which they are located. Maine Audubon's furnace is heavily insulated so that most heat generated by combustion is carried out of the stove in the flue gases. The flue gases and heat are ducted over the length of the gravel storage bed used by the solar collector. Heat is transfered to the gravel from the flue by blowing air across the pipes and then on through the gravel.

The flue pipes are standard 8″ ribbed and galvanized steel culvert pipe. The heat exchange system of the culverts and gravel bed causes the temperature of the flue gases to drop from as high as 1,000°F to 150° as they move through the 140′ length of pipe suspended above the rock storage bed.

A stack draft inducing fan is necessary because the air is so cool at the end of its passage through the heat exchanger that it no longer has enough buoyancy to continue rising out of the chimney.

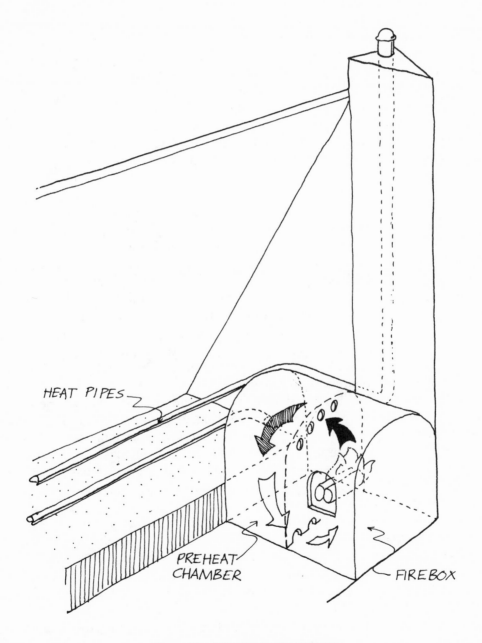

Figure 16   WOOD STOVE DETAIL

The heat exchanging flue pipes also give the Maine Audubon furnace an unusual extra source of heat. In all other stoves, water contained in wood is converted to steam and expelled out the chimney. Under the Maine Audubon system, this steam is allowed to condense within the flue pipe as heat is removed in the exchangers. When the steam condenses from gas to liquid, energy is released. This energy is captured because the transformation occurs in the heat exchanger, instead of in the outside air. The liquid thus condensed is ducted out of the flue and disposed.

2. Efficient combustion.

Other wood furnaces control excess heat output by reducing the amount of air the fire receives. Cutting down on air supply to the wood, however, greatly reduces the efficiency of combustion and therefore reduces the heat output of the furnace per pound of wood consumed as fuel. A reduction in efficiency also means that air pollution is increased because incompletely combusted material escapes as stack gases.

The Maine Audubon furnace does not need to control heat output because excess heat is stored in the gravel until needed by the building. The furnace is allowed to burn rapidly at high temperatures by injecting excess air into the furnace. This insures complete combustion and a minimum of air pollution. A single burn of the wood stove with 100 lbs. of hardwood should provide enough heat for an average winter's day.

Air is injected into the stove by using the "venturi" effect. This principle specifies that high velocity flow will create a partial vacuum on the edge of its path that tends to suck flow streams along. A simple example of this is a truck passing at high speed tending to pull other cars along with it for a brief moment while it passes because it creates a vacuum behind itself as it moves.

The furnace takes advantage of this principle to insure complete combustion by shooting a high velocity but small stream of air into the fire box. Uncombusted gases are sucked back into the fire to be completely burned as the illustration shows.

A forced-air heating system of conventional design is used to transfer heat from the storage area to the building in response to automatic thermostatic controls. Rooms are individually zoned to allow the greatest flexibility in heating and to allow for the conservation of heat in unoccupied rooms.

The building has been designed to make the greatest possible use of energy conservation techniques. Among the design characteristics are the use of triple pane glass windows throughout the building, thermal curtains, a vestibule designed to reduce infiltration, 6" fiberglass insulation in the walls, and 8" fiberglass in the ceiling area. It is projected that these design elements, coupled with a polyurethane membrane on the walls of the building, will reduce infiltration to a rate below one air change per hour. This is considerably below the average of eight to ten air changes in traditional commercial buildings. The projected heating needs will be only 1772 BTU's per hour, a very low per square foot heating need, by commercial or residential standards.

It is estimated that the solar system will provide about 70% of the overall heating needs of the building with the remaining 30% taken up by the wood heating system. This would be equivalent to approximately three cords of dry oak. At $50 a cord, the cost for wood will be $160 a year.

Electricity to operate the induced draft fans in the wood stove is calculated to be 470 kw. hr. per year or approximately $25 at current rates. The solar system will take somewhat more energy to circulate air through the rock storage and collector area. Annual operating requirements are projected at 2134 kw. hr. per year with a safety factor of 1.5%. The cost at current rates would be $151.83 per year.

The total electric energy needed to operate the building heating system will be approximately 2604 kw. hr. per year. The cost overall, at current rates, will be $345.23 per year.

A windmill-powered water pump will provide water from the well and a Clivus Multrum toilet system, which uses no water, will be installed. The Swedish designed Clivus Multrum consists of a relatively compact fiberglass "digestion chamber" which stores wastes as they slowly decompose. At the end of a two year cycle, a few bushels of odorless organic humus are produced each year and can be recycled to gardens.

As was mentioned earlier, there is no reason why any of these systems could not be scaled down to single family residence size. After this building has operated for an entire heating season, conclusive results should be available to verify (or modify) the projections of the building's designers.

Anyone wishing more information about this project may obtain a Technical Information Package, including a set of half-size original architectural plans and full engineering documentation of the solar and wood-heating system, by sending $8 to: Maine Audubon Society, 53 Baxter Boulevard, Portland, Maine 04101.

BIBLIOGRAPHY

Anderson, Bruce. SOLAR ENERGY IN BUILDING DESIGN. 1976
Available from Total Environmental Action, Harrisville, New Hampshire 03450 $28.
Very up-to-date, practically applicable (and researched!) material.

Commoner, Barry. THE POVERTY OF POWER. New York: Alfred Knopf, 1976.

Clark Wilson. ENERGY FOR SURVIVAL. Garden City, New York: Anchor Press, 1974.
$4.95. An exhaustive reference book containing a wealth of pertinent statistics.

Gay, Larry. HEATING WITH WOOD. Charlotte, Vermont: Garden Way Publishing, 1974.
$3.95. Interesting reading.

Havens, David. THE WOODBURNER'S HANDBOOK. Brunswick, Maine: Harpswell Press, 1973.
Available from the publishers at Simpsons Point Road, Brunswick, Maine 04011, $2.95. Good information on buying and fixing up old stoves and ranges, and obtaining wood.

Kern, Ken. THE OWNER BUILT HOME. Oakhurst, California: Owner Built Publications, 1961

Kern, Ken. THE OWNER BUILT HOMESTEAD. Oakhurst, California: Owner Built Publications
Both of the above are radical guides to economical building and living.

Shelton, Jay, et al. THE WOODBURNER'S ENCYCLOPEDIA. Vermont Crossroads Press, 1976
May be obtained from Vermont Energy Resources, Box 1, Fiddler's Green, Waitsfield, Vermont 05673. Bumper stickers reading "Wood Energy" may also be obtained from this source. Bumper stickers reading "Woodburners Have More Fun" may be obtained from Kristia Associates, Portland, Maine. Bumper stickers reading "Split Wood Not Atoms" may be obtained from New England Coalition on Nuclear Pollution, Box 675, Brattleboro, Vermont 05301.

United States Department of Agriculture, Forest Service. THE OUTLOOK FOR TIMBER IN THE U.S., 1973
Available from the United States Government Printing Office, Washington, D.C. 20402. $3.25. Good source of statistics but not current - you practically need a forester's education to make anything out of this.

BIBLIOGRAPHY

United States Department of Agriculture, Forest Products Laboratory. THEORIES OF THE COMBUSTION OF WOOD AND ITS CONTROL. 1958
Available from the United States Department of Agriculture, Madison 5, Wisconsin. Technical chemistry text.

Gillespie, John, ed. HOW TO PLAN AND BUILD FIREPLACES. Menlo Park, California: Lane Books, 1973

Energy Policy Project of the Ford Foundation. A TIME TO CHOOSE: AMERICA'S ENERGY FUTURE. Cambridge, Massachusetts: Bollinger Publishing Co., 1974
Excellent recommendations and comments for national energy policy. Now over two years old but still very fresh and applicable and in need of serious government application.

Anderson, Bruce, ed. SOLAR AGE MAGAZINE. Vernon, New Jersey: Solar Vision, Inc.
Available from Solar Vision, Inc. Box 288, Route 515, Vernon, New Jersey 67462. $20 for twelve issues. Includes articles on woodheating and building design.

Cook, James R., ed. WOODBURNING QUARTERLY. Minneapolis, Minnesota
Available from 8009 34th Avenue South, Minneapolis, Minnesota 55420.

INDEX

Bold figures indicate illustrations.

INDEX

Flue Stopper